*"I don't want you lying to my mom."*

"What are you talking about?"

Rico brushed his lips across hers, once, twice.

Molly sucked in her breath but didn't move. Didn't speak, didn't stop him. Instead, she placed a tentative hand on his chest, then slowly gripped the lapel of his jacket—to steady herself, no doubt. Or maybe to draw him closer?

Her lips parted before she came to her senses and pulled away. "What in the world was that all about?"

"Tell my mother that I'm rude or a cynical jerk. Tell her I'm a die-hard bachelor, that I'm stubborn and cocky and too set in my ways. But don't tell her there's no chemistry between us," he added, flashing her a rebel grin. "Because *that*, sweet Molly, would be a bold-faced lie."

Dear Reader,

So—it's the new year. Time for new beginnings. And we at Special Edition take that very seriously, so this month we offer the first of six books in our new FAMILY BUSINESS continuity. In it, a family shattered by tragedy finds a way to rebuild. *USA TODAY* bestselling author Susan Mallery opens the series with *Prodigal Son,* in which the son who thought he'd rid himself of the family business is called back to save it—with the help of his old (figuratively speaking) and beautiful business school nemesis. Don't miss it!

It's time for new beginnings for reader favorite Patricia Kay also, who this month opens CALLIE'S CORNER CAFÉ, a three-book miniseries centered around a small-town restaurant that serves as home base for a group of female friends. January's kickoff book in the series is *A Perfect Life,* which features a woman who thought she had the whole life-plan thing down pat—until fate told her otherwise. Talk about reinventing yourself! Next up, Judy Duarte tells the story of a marriage-phobic man, his much-married mother…and the wedding planner who gets involved with them both, in *His Mother's Wedding.* Jessica Bird continues THE MOOREHOUSE LEGACY with *His Comfort and Joy.* For years, sweet, small-town Joy Moorehouse has fantasized about arrogant, big-city Grayson Bennett.… Are those fantasies about to become reality? In *The Three-Way Miracle* by Karen Sandler, three people—a woman, a man and a child—greatly in need of healing, find all they need in each other. And in Kate Welsh's *The Doctor's Secret Child,* what starts out as a custody battle for a little boy turns into a love story. You won't be able to put it down.…

Enjoy them all—and don't forget next month! It's February, and you know what that means.…

Here's to new beginnings.…

Gail Chasan
Senior Editor

Please address questions and book requests to:
Silhouette Reader Service
U.S.: 3010 Walden Ave., P.O. Box 1325, Buffalo, NY 14269
Canadian: P.O. Box 609, Fort Erie, Ont. L2A 5X3

# HIS MOTHER'S WEDDING

## *JUDY DUARTE*

Silhouette

**SPECIAL EDITION**

Published by Silhouette Books

America's Publisher of Contemporary Romance

To Virginia Collis, the very first reader to take
pen in hand and tell me she liked my books.

Virginia, this story is for you.
I hope you give it a thumbs-up, too!

 SILHOUETTE BOOKS

ISBN 0-373-24731-1

HIS MOTHER'S WEDDING

Copyright © 2006 by Judy Duarte

Visit Silhouette Books at www.eHarlequin.com

**Printed in U.S.A.**

**Books by Judy Duarte**

Silhouette Special Edition

*Cowboy Courage* #1458
*Family Practice* #1511
*Almost Perfect* #1540
*Big Sky Baby* #1563
*The Virgin's Makeover* #1593
*Bluegrass Baby* #1598
*The Rich Man's Son* #1634
*\*Hailey's Hero* #1659
*\*Their Secret Son* #1667
*\*Their Unexpected Family* #1676
*\*Worth Fighting For* #1684
*\*The Matchmakers' Daddy* #1689
*\*His Mother's Wedding* #1731

Silhouette Romance

*A Bride for a
    Blue-Ribbon Cowboy* #1776

Silhouette Books

*Double Destiny*
"Second Chance"

\*Bayside Bachelors

---

## JUDY DUARTE

An avid reader who enjoys a happy ending, Judy Duarte loves to create stories of her own. When she's not cooped up in her writing cave, she's spending time with her some-what enormous, but delightfully close family.

Judy makes her home in California with her personal hero, their youngest son and a cat named Mom. "Sharing a name with the family pet gets a bit confusing," she admits. "Especially when the cat decides to curl up in a secluded cubbyhole and hide. I'm not sure what the neighbors think when my son walks up and down the street calling for Mom."

You can write to Judy c/o Silhouette Books, 233 Broadway, Suite 1001, New York, NY 10237. Or you can contact her through her Web site at: www.judyduarte.com.

Mr. Rico Garcia
requests the honor of your presence
at the marriage of his mother

Colette Marie Garcia

to

Dr. Daniel Osterhout

Saturday, the third of June
at two o'clock in the afternoon
Westlake Community Church
Westlake, New York

Reception to follow

## Chapter One

"Hi, baby. It's me. Where've you been lately? Are we still on for this weekend?"

As he listened to his voice mail, Rico Garcia leaned back in his tufted leather desk chair and blew out a sigh.

Damn. He and Suzette had a date on Saturday, and he'd completely forgotten. Talk about a subconscious desire to cut bait and run.

Not that he'd been stringing her along.

On the day they'd met, he'd made it clear he didn't commit, and she'd eagerly agreed to his terms. Now, two months later, she was having second thoughts.

And so was he.

Not about committing, though. About their relationship.

He opened the file drawer on the lower right side of his desk where he kept it full of candy and reached into an open bag of Reese's Pieces. He had a stash of goodies in the glove box of his car, too.

As a kid, he spent the bulk of his allowance on sweets. But after his step-dad was shot, and the proceeds of the life insurance policy dwindled, any money Rico could scavenge went toward rent and utility bills.

He grabbed a handful of the autumn-colored candies, popped them into his mouth and savored the peanut butter taste. The first time he'd eaten them was back in the early eighties, after watching *E.T. The Extra-Terrestrial* at the Sunday matinee. And they'd been one of his favorites ever since.

After listening to the rest of his messages and making the appropriate return calls, he pulled the Rolodex across his mahogany desk.

He needed to break things off with Suzette. But he wouldn't do it on a night she was expecting dinner and a sleepover. He'd just have to cancel their date. Then, at the beginning of the week, he'd stop by her house and tell her she ought to look for someone who wanted the same things out of life that she did.

As he flipped through the tabs, he found V and looked for Vio…Vya…

What the hell was the name of the company Suzette worked for?

As a private investigator, details like that *never* slipped his mind. But sometimes, when it came to relationships with women, his brain didn't work the same way. The selective-memory thing bothered him a bit, though. Probably because he prided himself on the ability to recall trivial details about a case.

There was a real rush when an investigation struck pay dirt, as most of his did.

Most—but not all of them.

He glanced at the only photograph that sat on his desk, a dark-metal-framed picture of Frank Stafford standing beside his 1963 Corvette Stingray—tuxedo-black, with a split back window and a three-twenty-seven-cubic-inch fuel-injection engine.

The photo had been taken right after Frank bought the vintage vehicle. That was a year before his stepfather had died in a hunting "accident," a case Rico hadn't been able to solve. One that wouldn't grow cold until his memory of Frank died.

He glanced out the window, catching a view of the Empire State Building. It was cloudy and overcast today. Rain, most likely. He hoped to get out of there before the storm hit, but that wasn't going to happen. He still had work to do.

Rico owned and operated a highly successful private investigative firm. Garcia and Associates was and always would be his baby, his life. He'd built the elite and discreet agency to the level where he had a top-notch office staff and the most skilled and professional private investigators in the business. He could probably take some time off—if he wanted to. But he thrived on having the focus his work provided.

The intercom light flashed, then buzzed.

Beep. "Mr. Garcia?"

"Yes, Margie."

"Your mother is on line three."

"Thanks." Rico let the Rolodex cards slip through his fingers. He hadn't talked to his mom in weeks and hoped everything was all right. He worried about her sometimes.

No, make that *a lot.*

He pressed the lit button on line three and took his mother's call. "Hey, stranger. What's up?"

"Oh, Rico. You'll never believe what happened." His mom's voice, while innately cheerful, held an even more upbeat tone than usual. "I have wonderful news."

"What'd you do? Hit the lottery?"

"No. It's much better than that."

Better than money?

He didn't like the sound of that already. He'd spent the first twenty years of his life living with and looking after his sweet, softhearted but gullible mother. And her "good news" always put his skeptical nature on alert.

She'd better not be talking about another pyramid

scheme she'd been roped into. The last time, he'd had to put some pressure on the guy who'd preyed on divorcées and widows, making him give the money back. Then he'd turned the sorry son of a bitch in to the local police.

His mother had gotten her investment back—*that* time.

"Listen, I've only got a couple of minutes before my next appointment, Mom. Why don't you just tell me your good news?"

"Well, all right. I've met the most wonderful man in the world. And I've fallen in love."

Oh, for cripes sake. *Again?*

It's not as though Rico didn't want to see his mom happy, but he'd been through enough heartbreak with her as it was. He just wished she'd stop believing that some Romeo was going to ride into her life and carry her away to a castle in the sky.

She, more than anyone, ought to know that.

"Rico?" she asked. "Did you hear me?"

"Yeah, Mom. I heard you."

"You're not excited?"

Hell no, he wasn't excited. At fifty-two, his mother had been married four times already. When was she going to put away those fairy-tale dreams and call it quits?

But damn, he couldn't snap at her like that. She'd probably start crying. And Lord knew he couldn't handle her tears.

He leaned back in his chair, leather creaking. "You

know I want to see you happy, Mom. But who is this guy?"

"His name is Daniel Osterhout. He's a dentist. And he's my soul mate."

A soul mate, huh? Well, that's a term she'd never used before. Couldn't she just sleep with the guy? Why did she have to marry every man she was attracted to?

"How long have you known him?"

"Nearly a month."

"That's not very long."

"It seems as though I've known him forever."

Rico sighed.

"Oh, come on, honey," she said softly. "I understand your skepticism, but Daniel is different. You'll see. And someday you're going to meet someone special, too."

Rico rolled his eyes heavenward in a God-help-me way. He loved his mom, he really did. But he wished she wasn't so trusting. Her heart had been tromped on many times in the past. And she certainly didn't deserve the pain and disappointment she continually set herself up for.

Couldn't she be just a little more realistic about love?

"Daniel and I have decided to get married in June," she added, a singsong enthusiasm resonating in her voice. "What do you think?"

Truthfully?

Rico thought it was a joke to have a big hoopla, especially under the circumstances. Hell, this guy would be her fifth husband. "When you say wedding, you're talking about a little ceremony down at the courthouse with a justice of the peace and a couple of witnesses, right?"

"Well, actually, Daniel and I would like a church wedding, an organist, a few close friends and family. That sort of thing."

As far as Rico was concerned, *that sort of thing* sounded *way* too involved. But what the hell. "I guess there's nothing wrong with June, as long as you're sure about this."

"I've never been more sure about anything." She undoubtedly thought that would make him feel better.

It didn't.

"Of course, I may need to borrow a little money," she added. "The bride is supposed to put on the wedding, and I might come up a bit short."

They both knew she wouldn't be "borrowing" any money, but Rico would step up to the plate. He always did. Heck, he'd never been able to deny his mom anything.

Ever since his father died, it had been just the two of them—well, other than a progression of stepfathers who for some reason or another swung in and out of their lives as if they where traveling through a revolving door. Each one had offered a lonely mother and child the promise and hope of a family and then provided them everything but.

He glanced at Frank's picture, picked it up. Okay, so

that one hadn't hurt them on purpose, but his unexpected death had left them alone and hurting just the same.

"All right," he told his mom. "I'll spring for the wedding if you'll try and keep it small."

They both knew Rico wasn't a cheapskate. He could well afford a fancy wingding. But he wasn't into dog-and-pony shows.

"Oh, honey," she said, her voice getting all soft and mushy. "You're so good to me."

"Yeah? Well, you've been pretty good to me, too."

They'd been through a lot together—more than their share of pain and struggles. There was a time when they'd both had to work to keep a roof over their heads, and Rico hadn't even hit his teen years.

"I love you."

"Me, too," he told her. But the words weren't necessary. She knew he loved her unconditionally even if she frustrated the hell out of him at times.

"Are you sure about this?" he asked again.

"Absolutely."

Dead silence.

Then he blew out a sigh and reeled in his ever-present cynicism the best he could. "Okay. Then I'm happy for you." Well, not exactly happy. Resigned, he supposed.

But that didn't mean he wouldn't do a little background check on Prince Charming, D.D.S.

He picked up a pen. "What did you say this guy's name was?"

"Daniel Osterhout."

"Spell it."

"You're not writing that down, are you?"

"Humor me."

"You're not going to have one of your investigators dig into his background, are you?"

"Of course not." Rico wasn't about to pass this job on to anyone else.

She spelled out the name.

"Is that German?"

"On his father's side."

"So where did you meet him?"

"I found a coupon in the *Dollarsaver* offering a free dental exam and X-rays to new patients at his office in Westlake, so I called and made an appointment. I know you don't believe in this sort of thing, but it was love at first sight."

In a dental chair? How romantic.

*Open your mouth and say "aah."*

*Aah…ooh, baby.*

"Nope, I'm a skeptic when it comes to stuff like that, Mom. But I'm glad you're happy." He just hoped she'd stay that way.

As an adolescent, he'd pinned his hopes on each man she'd brought into their lives. And after weathering each disappointment, he'd become tough and callused when it came to buying into the fairy tale of love. But he'd managed to survive, to become strong.

His mom, on the other hand, had been a slow learner. And he was afraid that one more failed marriage, either through death, divorce or abandonment, would do her in rather than toughen her up.

"Daniel and I would like to take you out to dinner this weekend," she said.

Garcia and Associates, with offices in New York, Chicago and L.A., hadn't become a booming company without its owner working long, hard hours and pouring his blood, sweat and tears into the place. Rico couldn't just take off on a personal jaunt for the hell of it.

Okay, due to the agency's success, that wasn't *entirely* true anymore.

"I don't know if I can get away," he lied, hoping that if he dragged his feet, her budding romance would blow over before he had to meet the guy.

"Oh, come on, honey. You put in too many hours as it is. Besides, you've hired some new investigators, like that man you call Cowboy. So surely you can drive up here for a day."

He glanced at his calendar. Once he gave Suzette a call, he'd have some free time this weekend. "All right. I'll come down on Saturday afternoon. We can have dinner, I'll meet your dental soul mate, then I'll head back to the city."

"You can also stay the night in my spare room. I'll make homemade biscuits and sausage gravy in the morning."

"Nothing like twisting my arm. The last woman I was seeing tried to get me on a health kick—tofu, wheat germ and a bunch of other crap—so I'm ready to bolt."

"You're between ladies right now?"

Warning bells went off. There was no way he wanted his mother fixing him up with anyone. *No way.* She thought the perfect woman for him was someone a lot like herself, someone with her head in the clouds and her eye on true love forever.

And for some dumb reason, she couldn't get it in her mind that he'd quit believing in pipe dreams like marriage a long time ago. And not just because of his mother's marital history.

He had a friend, Mac McGuire, whose wife had tried to force him to give up being a cop, who'd tried to make him move to the suburbs and trade in his police cruiser for a minivan. They'd even had a kid together, which had only made things worse.

And then fate, as it was prone to do, threw Mac a nasty curve. He and his wife divorced, his son was later killed in a traffic accident and the resulting grief led to some heavy drinking, a misconduct charge at work....

Nope, he wouldn't set himself up for something like that.

"Listen," he told his mom. "I'm not looking for a date, if that's what you've got on your mind. But I'll come up and have dinner with you on Saturday. And if the biscuits-and-gravy deal is still on, I'll spend the night."

"I'm so glad. And by the way…"

Uh-oh. Rico instinctively braced himself.

"I have a good friend who needs a private investigator. And I thought…"

"You thought that I'd do it as a favor to you."

"You'll help her, won't you?"

Oh, he'd grumble a bit. But he'd do it, as he always did. His mother seemed to gravitate toward people who needed his services. And those "good friends" always expected him to investigate something or other as a courtesy. Shoot, the last one just wanted some genealogical information for a cross-stitch of her family tree, something she could have easily found online.

But what the hell.

Rico loved his mom—big old heart, rose-colored glasses and all. "What's the trouble this time?"

"My friend is trying to locate a younger sister she hasn't seen since they were children. It would mean so much to her. And to me."

"All right. I'll see what I can do."

"Good. I'll have her at my house on Saturday afternoon. Maybe she can join us for dinner."

Well, at least his mom wasn't trying to set him up with anyone.

When they said their goodbyes, Rico hung up the telephone, then resumed his search for Suzette's number.

If there was anything that made him even more determined to avoid commitments, it was a chat with his mother—God bless her sweet, ever-trusting heart.

Molly Townsend had never met a woman more like herself. Even the fact that Colette Garcia was old enough to be her mother hadn't stopped them from becoming good friends in a matter of weeks.

As Molly sat on the sofa in the small but cozy living room of the older woman's home, Colette poured them each a cup of tea from a delicate hand-painted china pot.

At five foot six and in her early fifties, Colette was a stylish and attractive woman, with dyed red hair, expressive blue eyes and an optimistic heart of gold.

"You know," Colette said, "I'm sure that Rico will love Daniel once he gets to know him. But having them meet for the first time has me a little nervous and on edge. Rico is so protective of me. Too much so, actually."

"I'm sure everything will go beautifully." Molly took the ivory-colored cup and saucer, noting the delicate lilac and green-leaf trim.

"You're probably right, but I'm glad you'll be going to dinner with us. I don't think Rico is too excited about me having a wedding, even though he agreed to pay for it. And I'm hoping you can explain to him how much this means to me. I've been married four times, but I've never been in love—not this deeply. Daniel and I are both making a lifetime commitment to each other and we want to do it right."

"I'll do whatever I can."

As a wedding consultant at Betty's Bridal Boutique, Molly had run into more than one perplexed father of the bride who didn't understand the emotional and symbolic importance of a wedding. Of course, she'd never had to deal with the *son* of a bride before.

"You know, Rico should be here anytime." The older woman glanced at her gold wristwatch, then grinned. "I'm so glad you're going to get a chance to meet him."

So was Molly. When Colette had first mentioned her son was the owner of a successful private investigative agency, she couldn't believe her luck. For years she'd wanted to find her younger sister but hadn't known where to start.

Colette insisted that Rico would be happy to do the legwork at no charge. But Molly wouldn't be comfortable with that. She would insist upon paying for his services. A reunion with her little sister would be worth any price.

"You know," Colette said, "Rico doesn't know where I'm coming from with Daniel. He'd be so much happier if he did. He really needs to find a nice girl and settle down."

Molly wondered if this was a setup. If so, it made her a tad uneasy, even though she was eager to find that special someone God created just for her, a prince among men. In fact, she usually looked forward to meeting potential mates, especially if they'd been recommended by a friend.

But Molly had a high set of standards not many men could fill. And from what she'd heard, she suspected Colette's son would fall short of her expectations.

"You know," Colette said, "I have a good feeling about you and Rico."

So this *was* a setup.

Molly took a sip of tea, her senses on alert. Her primary motive for meeting Rico was to talk to him about locating her sister. She would, of course, give him a chance—if she'd misjudged him and found him to be like his warmhearted, optimistic, family-oriented mother.

Time would tell, though.

Molly placed her cup and saucer on the coffee table, then reached for her notepad. "Do you want to discuss the wedding details over dinner or should we bring them up this afternoon?"

"Maybe we ought to wait until Daniel gets here. I'd really like him to be a part of this."

Molly nodded.

"You know," Colette said again, "you're going to love Rico."

"I hope so," Molly responded. "But there's something you need to understand. I'm open to meeting eligible bachelors, but I'm pretty fussy."

"And you should be."

Molly had to agree. She'd had a lousy example of home and family during the first twelve years of her life and she wasn't about to let history repeat itself. But she'd seen the best and worst of families.

Some people might not understand how a young woman with a lousy early childhood like Molly's could grow up and not become jaded and bitter.

Well, that was easy. Molly had Don and Barbara Townsend to thank for that.

Her foster parents had taught her that things always worked out for the best. That heroes like the Townsends existed. That love prevailed. And that—somewhere— her soul mate waited.

Colette patted Molly's knee with a light touch of the hand. "Well, picky or not, you're going to like my son." Then she led softly. "I know what you're probably thinking—every old crow thinks her baby's white as snow. But Rico is about the most handsome man who ever walked the face of the earth."

As far as Molly was concerned, a man's physical appearance wasn't anywhere near as important as his character. And she'd put plenty of thought into that conclusion.

In her heart she knew that she was looking for a guy who was a lot like Don Townsend, a man in touch with his feelings and understanding of hers. In many ways the sweet, slightly stooped, balding man had become a template for her dream mate.

Of course, when she allowed her fantasies to take flight, her future husband had a keen resemblance to Brad Pitt.

As the roar of a high-performance engine grew near, Colette placed her teacup and saucer on the glass-topped coffee table and stood. "Oh, good. He's here."

She'd recognized her son's vehicle?

Not that it mattered, but it sounded like some kind of race car.

All right, so Molly had failed to consider the style of vehicle Mr. Right ought to drive. But she couldn't imagine Don Townsend racing through town in a Porsche or a Ferrari.

"Will you excuse me for a minute?" Colette asked as she approached the front door.

"Sure." Molly brushed her palms across the black knit fabric of her simple but classic A-line dress.

Hope might spring eternal, but something told her Rico wouldn't be her type, no matter what his mother had said. His job as a private investigator in itself sent up a red flag.

She wanted someone with a nine-to-five job, a man who would spend time with his family in the evenings and on weekends. And she doubted Colette's son would ever be home.

His car sent up another flag.

What kind was it? The revved-up sound of the engine suggested speed and flash. A risk taker. An attention seeker.

A real turnoff, if you asked her.

But Molly was open-minded. Well, skeptical but unbiased. So she'd have to meet the man first.

As Colette went outside to greet her son, Molly couldn't quell a growing curiosity. So she made her way to the big bay window that looked out into the sub-urban tree-lined street and stood to the side, hidden behind the pale, cream-colored panel curtains.

Outside, a vintage Corvette, completely restored and as black as night, sat curbside behind her faded blue Toyota.

She continued to stare as a tall, dark-haired man climbed from the classic sports car, wearing a pair of sunglasses and a devilish smile.

He walked around his vehicle and stepped onto the sidewalk, dressed casually in a pair of black slacks and a white shirt with the sleeves rolled up. Everything about him shouted out *Flirt. Player.*

Yet a flurry of butterflies swept through Molly's tummy, and her heart slipped into a zippity-do-dah beat.

How crazy was that?

Especially when she'd never been attracted to the tall, dark and aren't-I-gorgeous type.

She could tell right now that she'd never want to be-come romantically involved with Rico Garcia.

But for some dumb reason, her hormones didn't seem to be listening.

## *Chapter Two*

At just after five o'clock Rico arrived at his mom's house—a small, two-bedroom tract home on a quiet street in Westlake Falls.

Three years ago, when the first phase of the development had been released, he'd surprised her by purchasing her a new house. She'd gotten over her shock and quickly set about hanging pictures and making it her own.

She'd not only decorated the inside but had done a great job with the landscape, too. The wood-and-wrought-iron bench on the lawn had been added since the last time he'd come to visit, and so had the concrete garden figurine—an angel, no doubt. Or maybe it was a cupid.

For as along as Rico could remember, his mom had had a talent for making a run-down shack feel like home.

Each time she moved into a place, she left her mark by setting a glass bowl of potpourri on the coffee table, framed photographs on the mantel, a vanilla-scented candle on the counter and other things like that. And if she knew Rico was stopping by, there would always be something cooking on the stove or baking in the oven.

He admired that about her, the ability to provide him a place where he could temporarily slip off his cloak of cynicism and hang it by the door.

Of course, this time he wouldn't be removing his "outerwear." He was going to need it to check out the new man in her life, to make sure his mom would be treated well—that she'd be appreciated, respected.

To him, that was a hell of a lot more important than being in love with her soul mate.

As Rico slowed in front of the house, he saw that his mom had parked her Ford Taurus at a diagonal, taking up the entire driveway. So he pulled his Corvette along the curb, behind a blue Toyota Corolla that had seen better years.

He sure hoped the Toyota didn't belong to Dr. Osterhout. If his mom was going to get married again, he wanted her husband to be able to support her in the manner she deserved. And he'd feel better if the dentist drove a late-model Mercedes or Lincoln.

His preliminary investigation showed the guy to be

on the up-and-up. But Rico still wasn't convinced. When it came to choosing men, at least the last couple of times, his mom's track record had been lousy.

Rico got out of his car and took another look at the Toyota. An artificial red rose was attached to the antenna with a ribbon, suggesting the driver couldn't always remember where he or she parked. The rear bumper had a few dings, not to mention a dented New York license plate. Dang. Maybe his car would be safer if he parked across the street.

"Hello, honey." His mom, dressed in black slacks and a lightweight gray sweater, stepped onto the front porch and met him in the driveway with a warm hug.

He inhaled the familiar scent of gardenias, a fragrance that belonged only to her.

"How was your drive?" she asked as she led him into the small white house.

"It wasn't bad." He nodded over his shoulder, toward the Toyota. "Whose car?"

"It's Molly's. I'll introduce you."

Oh, yeah. The lady who wanted to find her sister.

As they stepped into the living room that had been painted a pale green, Rico scanned the small, cozy interior, looking for his mom's friend.

Expecting a middle-aged woman, he was blindsided by a petite twenty-something blonde in the center of the room.

She stood about five-three and wore her shoulder-length hair in a classic style. A simple black knit dress stretched whisper-soft along each feminine curve.

Her smile sucked the air out of the room.

Had they been at a club in the city, he would have easily picked her out of the crowd and sidled up to her, asked if he could buy her a drink. Maybe taken her out on the dance floor. And if she'd been agreeable, they might have ended the night in bed.

But what was a woman like her doing at his mom's house?

"Rico," his mother said, "this is my friend Molly, the one I told you about."

Unbelievable. *This* was his mom's *friend?*

For a guy who prided himself on being prepared for the unexpected, Rico was damn near *gawking* at her. But damn, he'd always been partial to blondes.

He tried to rein in his surprise and extended an arm in greeting. "How do you do?"

"I'm fine, thank you." Molly took his hand. "It's nice to meet you."

Her skin was soft, cool. Her fingers delicate. Her nails unpolished, plain yet filed neatly. Silver heart charms dangled from a chain on her wrist.

His gaze locked on hers, and he studied her eyes, the brilliant shade of green, the tiny gold flecks. The thick, spiky lashes that didn't need mascara.

Shake it off, he reprimanded himself. This lady was a friend of his mom's, for God's sake. Looking for a husband and kids, no doubt.

In the past, his mom had tried to play matchmaker by

introducing him to women like Molly. But Rico hadn't taken the bait. Hopefully she'd learned her lesson, since it had been a while since she'd tried to set him up.

Molly flashed him another pretty smile that damn near knocked the wind out of him, then slowly pulled her fingers from his grasp.

Had he held her hand a few seconds too long? He hadn't meant to. But he wasn't going to stress about it. It had to happen to her all the time.

"Molly and I met when I was shopping at Betty's Bridal Boutique," his mom said.

Oh, yeah. The wedding. It had completely slipped his mind the moment he strode into the room and laid eyes on Molly.

They'd met at Betty's Bridal Boutique, huh? Had the pretty blonde been looking for a wedding dress, too?

That wouldn't surprise him. He imagined a lot of guys would want to stake a permanent claim on an attractive woman like her.

"And with Molly's help," his mom said, "I found the perfect dress. It's off-white, with a pearl-encrusted bodice. And it was on sale. It'll need alterations, but it's gorgeous."

"You bought the dress already?" he asked, unable to keep the surprise from his voice. "What if you change your mind?" Or to be more accurate, what if he managed to convince her she was jumping into things too quickly?

"Don't be silly son. I'm not going to change my mind. But I only put the dress on hold. I wanted you to see it first."

Rico glanced at Molly. A starry-eyed smile bore evidence of her support of the wedding. No wonder she and his mom were fast friends.

"You really ought to see the dress on her," Molly interjected. "It's perfect. And with the calla lilies she chose for her bouquet…"

Rico's turned to his mom. "I thought you said it was just going to be a small church ceremony."

"There are a lot of formalities to consider when planning a wedding, no matter what size. And Betty's offers a consultant to help with it all."

"You're talking to a wedding planner?" The surprised tone in his voice escalated in spite of his natural inclination to remain cool, in control of his emotions. Unaffected.

But for Pete's sake, she was getting carried away.

He never could understand how women could get so damn caught up in all that bridal fuss. It was like the senior prom, only more ostentatious and a complete waste of time, money and emotion.

No one would ever rope Rico into a formal ceremony, assuming he ever found a reason to get married in the first place. But women seemed to go nuts over all the pomp and circumstance. And the wedding vendors—or rather, bridal vultures—saw them coming a mile away. Hell, all anyone had to do was mention the word *wedding* and the price of flowers, bands, banquet halls and the rest of that crap tripled.

He knew. His buddy Mac had complained to him at length about it.

"Daniel and I plan to keep the guest list under a hundred," his mom said.

Hell, even that sounded like a circus to Rico. "I thought you were going to keep things *simple. Small.*"

"We are, but there's a lot of etiquette involved, and Daniel and I want things to be done right." His mom lobbed a smile at her pretty, young friend. "Molly has been a godsend, especially since I've never had a *real* wedding before."

Rico tore his gaze from his mother, then looked at Molly, realizing she was much more than a pretty face. He didn't mean that as a compliment either. "Don't tell me you're the wedding consultant?"

"Yes," Molly said, "I am."

Damn. She probably worked on commission and had spotted his mom as an easy mark. He crossed his arms and shifted his weight to one foot. "Do you mind if we backpedal just a bit?"

"All right," his mom said. "Maybe I should start at the beginning."

"Good idea." His mother's explanations usually took a while, so he glanced at the only chair in the room. "Do you mind if I take a seat?"

"Of course not." His mom plopped down in the

green-and-lavender-plaid easy chair, leaving the coordinating floral sofa for Rico and Molly to share.

For a moment he got a strange sense that he was being set up, and not just with his mother's wedding. But maybe he was wrong. Maybe it was just his response to the unwelcome attraction he was feeling to his mother's wedding planner. In which case, designating pretty Molly as the enemy ought to take the edge off that.

"I already told you about meeting Daniel and falling in love with him," his mom said, her eyes glistening.

When Rico stole a glance at Molly, he saw her smiling and getting all misty-eyed, too. What was with women? Or at least these two? He couldn't find anything sentimental about a wedding, especially someone's *fifth*.

Molly sat on the edge of the cushion and tugged at the hem of her dress, making sure it reached her knees.

They were lovely knees, he realized. Nice legs, too.

But they were the knees and legs of the adversary, his mom's matrimonial cheerleader.

"Three weeks ago," his mom began, "I stopped by Betty's Bridal Boutique to look at dresses and to get some information about weddings. And that's when I met Molly." She blessed her young friend with a grin. "We hit it off immediately and had lunch together the next day. We have a lot in common in spite of our age difference."

Stars in their eyes, for one thing.

"I told you about Molly," his mom added. "Remember? On the telephone. And you agreed to help her find her sister."

So what was this—an attack from all sides?

They had him squirming in his seat—first with the wedding his mom didn't need, then with the free investigative work.

He hoped to hell he'd been mistaken about the cupid stuff.

Inadvertently he slid a peek at Molly's lap, where her hands rested primly. Her fingers were bare—not a diamond ring or a gold band in sight.

Great.

"Son, why don't I get you something to drink? I have iced tea, orange-mango juice, wine...."

"I'd like a scotch," Rico told her, thinking he'd better relax and not allow his emotions to get the better of him. Damn, this was going to be a hell of a long evening.

"Molly?" his mom asked. "How about you?"

The attractive blonde glanced at her bracelet, which he realized was actually a wristwatch.

"A glass of wine would be nice," she said.

When his mother disappeared, Rico leaned back in his seat, determined to take control of the conversation. "First of all, you can put down your pom-poms, Mollyanna."

"Excuse me?" Her tone was sharp, spunky, her spine ramrod straight.

He'd offended her, he supposed. And for a moment he thought about apologizing, starting over. But the physical attraction that didn't seem to be abating put him at a disadvantage. So he took the offense rather than the defense.

"Let's get something straight. I agreed to pay for this wedding. And it's not a matter of cost—I'd give my mom the moon if I could. But she's been married four times already. And I think under the circumstances things should be quiet and discreet."

Molly turned to face him, the hem of her dress sliding up her leg, revealing more skin than she probably realized and prompting him to swallow another urge to apologize and slip into a defensive stance.

"There's been a lot of heartbreak in your mother's past," she said. "And she deserves to be happy. Dr. Osterhout and your mom are truly in love."

Rico tried not to roll his eyes, but he couldn't hold back an exasperated sigh. "I hope you're right, but I'm a realist. I've seen the seedy side of life too often—first-hand as a kid, when I was a cop and sometimes when I'm investigating a case. And I've seen some of my mom's marriages. I don't believe in fairy tales and happy ever afters."

Her gaze dropped to her hands, then back to him, as though she felt sorry for him for some stupid reason. But she didn't need to. He'd come out on top. And he was stronger and tougher because of it.

So he brushed her sympathy aside. "There were only two men who deserved my mother's love and faith—my dad and my stepfather, Frank Stafford. And they died, leaving her heartbroken."

The other two husbands weren't worth mentioning.

"Your mom loved your father and Frank with a passion, and their deaths were hard on her."

"I know they were. So you'll have to excuse me for not getting all excited about her loving someone with a passion again." Rico hadn't ever known his dad, since he'd died in a five-car pileup on the Jersey Turnpike when Rico had been a baby. But he'd known—and adored—Frank, who'd entered their lives when Rico was in the first grade. But five years later Frank had been shot in a mysterious hunting "accident."

"Your mom said that Frank's death had been hard on you."

That wasn't true. Frank's death had been *devastating* to them both, but Rico had sucked it up when his mom hadn't been able to.

But then again, at the time Rico had focused on the details and questions surrounding Frank's death. Even as a kid Rico had known hunters got accidentally shot— but not while hunting on private property when supposedly no one else was around.

"Your mom was brokenhearted when Frank died," Molly added.

As if Rico didn't remember. He'd been crushed, too.

Frank had been the kind of father—step or otherwise—any child would love to have. The problem was, Frank's death had left them alone again. There'd been a small insurance policy that time, but when the money had run out, his mom had been forced to go back to work and Rico had become a latchkey kid.

But hey, that was okay. He'd learned to be tough, to take care of himself. And to look after his mom, too.

Rico had only been twelve, but he'd earned a little cash by doing odd jobs, like sweeping storefronts and picking up trash. And together they'd been able to keep a roof over their heads and food on the table.

"Sometimes," Molly said, "when a person is hurting and gets involved in another relationship too soon, it can lead to disaster."

Now she was talking. Rico sat up straight. "That's exactly what happened when my mom hooked up with Tom Crenshaw."

Colette had met the photocopier repairman while she'd been working for a temp agency, and he'd swept her off her feet—something that could easily happen when walking on clouds instead of solid ground.

Crenshaw had talked a good story, but after the two of them got married, he got bored.

"She told me he ran off with a college student," Molly said.

"Yeah. A liberal-studies major who moonlighted at a topless bar."

"That's too bad," Molly said, her voice soft, sympathetic.

"No, it wasn't. My mom was better off without him. And she was better off without number four, too."

That one had been a used-car salesman with a gambling problem.

"At least she asked him to leave," Molly said, her voice reflecting her rose-colored worldview.

"It's too bad she didn't boot his butt out of the house before he pissed away the bulk of everything she'd managed to save over the years."

"So she made a couple of mistakes. That doesn't mean she should suffer by being alone for the rest of her life."

"What's the matter with being alone?" he asked her.

She didn't answer, which made him think that she lived alone and disliked it. That in the evening she watched chick flicks, as his mom was prone to do, which probably was the reason they both thought they were missing out on something.

But he shook off his curiosity. It didn't take a high-priced psychologist to figure out he and Molly weren't suited. No matter how partial he was to blondes, no matter how attracted he was to her.

So Rico reverted back to the previous conversation about his mom's lousy choice of men, particularly her last husband. "If I ever get my hands on that guy, he's dog meat."

"You'd hurt him?" Molly's brow furrowed as though she thought Rico was some kind of ax murderer.

"I probably won't get the chance to have words with him or lay a hand on him. From what I found out, more than one shady bookie had it in for him. And chances are he's sleeping in the Hudson."

She clicked her tongue, like a teacher who was disappointed with one of her young students, then blew out a weary—no, make that a sympathetic—sigh. "After all your mother's been through, I'd think you'd like to see her happy."

"Hey, there's nothing I'd like better. But I *don't* want to see her hurt. *Again.*"

"Neither do I, but it'll be different this time. Dr. Osterhout is a wonderful man. Wait until you meet him." Mollyanna flashed him a hope-filled smile.

Damn. Talk about someone having a sunny attitude. "You're a lot like my mom."

She flashed him another smile. "Thank you."

He hadn't meant it as a compliment, but she hadn't picked up on that.

For a moment she plucked at the hem of her dress, then glanced up. Her emotion-laden gaze snagged his, making him almost feel guilty about something he should have said or done. "Your mom told me you might be able to help find my sister."

He shrugged. "My mom sometimes asks me to do a favor for her friends."

"I don't expect a free ride." Sincerity rang out in her voice. "I have some money put aside to pay for your services."

That old car outside, with the dents near the bumper, suggested she couldn't even pay *attention*.

But before Rico could come up with a response that wasn't cynical, his mother swept into the room carrying a tray with two wineglasses and a glass of scotch.

"I'm sorry for taking so long. But while I was in the kitchen, I gave Daniel a call on his cell phone. He's on his way over here now." She placed the tray on the glass-topped coffee table, next to a crystal bowl filled with her signature potpourri. "I hope you two had a chance to chat."

Molly offered her friend a smile but bit her tongue. She didn't know what she'd been expecting when Rico Garcia sauntered into his mother's living room, but certainly not a tall, dark hunk.

Colette had been right about him being handsome.

Okay, so her unmarried son was drop-dead gorgeous, with that thick head of dark hair, those golden-brown eyes and a dazzling smile that sent Molly's pulse skyrocketing.

He also had one of those avowed-bachelor auras, with a you-can-trust-me-baby dimple in his cheek and an I'll-call-you-in-a-couple-of-days smile.

No, Rico Garcia was a heartbreak waiting to happen.

He was also cynical and rude.

She'd wanted to pop him in the chops when he'd called her Mollyanna. As if being optimistic was a bad thing rather than an asset.

So why was she still having a hard time keeping her eyes off him? And why did her heart do somersaults each time he branded her with a gaze?

"We chatted a bit," Rico admitted as he picked up his glass and took a slow, steady drink.

They'd chatted long enough for her to know that Rico wanted to put a damper on his mom's wedding plans. And that when it came to romance, he had a pessimistic streak that ran from the tips of his black, curly hair to the bottoms of his snazzy Italian-leather shoes.

And long enough for her to peg him a ladies' man, a flirt and the kind of bachelor she steered clear of.

But they hadn't talked nearly enough. Molly was eager to discuss Lori, to give the private investigator what little information she had. To find out if there was any way to locate her younger sister.

As they each nursed their drinks, Molly couldn't help gazing at Rico when he wasn't looking. There was something magnetic about the guy. Something compelling. Something she'd have to guard against, which shouldn't be too difficult. In spite of being a romantic at heart, Molly wasn't stupid.

"We have dinner reservations at Antonio's," Colette said. "I hope six o'clock is all right with you."

"The sooner the better." Rico leaned back into the

sofa cushion and stretched out his legs. "I only had a bagel and coffee for breakfast and worked through lunch."

Molly was hungry, too. And she'd heard some nice things about Antonio's. The classy restaurant was under new management and had hired a chef who was supposedly incredible.

The telephone rang and Colette answered. Her face brightened, and Molly suspected it was Daniel on the line.

In spite of Rico's concern, Molly truly believed that Colette couldn't have fallen for a nicer man. Or for one who would treat her better.

"Of course I understand," Colette said. "But why don't I meet you at your office? I can sit in the waiting room, then we can drive to Antonio's together."

Molly had no idea what Daniel was saying, but Colette's side of the conversation gave her a clue.

"Not at all, dear. I'm sure Rico and Molly won't mind riding together."

We wouldn't? Molly slid a glance at Rico, saw his furrowed brow and suspected he might have a few qualms himself.

And she couldn't blame him. This whole dinner thing was beginning to look suspiciously like a romantic setup. And if it was, Colette had better scrap that star-crossed plan right away.

"Of course, Daniel. I'll leave as soon as I put on

some lipstick and get my purse. I can be at your office in fifteen minutes." Colette hung up the telephone, plopped her hands on the armrests of her chair and grinned. "I suppose I'll have to get used to calls like that. One of Daniel's patients has a dental emergency, and he can't meet us here."

Molly supposed it could be true. But why did she feel as if she were being railroaded? Did Colette really think her son needed a woman like Molly?

That couldn't be further from the truth.

Still, when she stole another peek at Rico and caught him studying her, her heart jumped and her pulse went a little screwy.

Darn it. She had her future all mapped out, and a man like Rico Garcia wasn't a part of it. She needed someone with a predictable schedule, someone who looked forward to spending evenings and weekends at home with the family. Someone who'd be willing to turn in his sports car for a minivan.

Of course, Molly *did* need Rico to help her find her sister.

Maybe she could talk to him about Lori when they rode together—an upside to Colette's matchmaking, she decided.

"Do you know where Antonio's is?" Colette asked her son.

"Yeah. It's on the corner of Ninth and Westlake Boulevard, isn't it?"

"No. It's on Raymond, just off Jefferson Parkway. Near the bookstore."

"I'll find it." Rico set his nearly full glass of scotch on the tray that rested on the coffee table. Then he got up from the sofa and looked at Molly. "I don't know about you, but I'm starving."

He seemed to be taking this all in stride, so why shouldn't she?

She placed her wineglass on the tray, then reached for her purse, slipped the shoulder strap over her arm, grabbed her trusty day planner and stood. "I can drive. I know where the restaurant is."

"No, that's okay," he said. "I don't like sitting in the passenger seat."

She didn't suppose he did.

As he placed a hand on the small of her back, a jolt of heat shot clear through her.

Oh, for goodness sake, how could his touch have that kind of effect on her when he was definitely Mr. Wrong?

As he escorted her out the door and to his car, she couldn't help commenting about an article she'd recently read in a women's magazine. "They say you tell a lot about people by the cars they drive."

He glanced at her Toyota. "That's what I'm afraid of."

In spite of the warmth from his touch, her backbone stiffened. "What's that supposed to mean? I can afford a better car, but I've been saving my money to pay for a private investigator."

"I wasn't sizing up your bank account, just your driving skill." He nodded toward the rear of her car, where the trunk had been dented.

"I bought that car used, and it came that way. I could have paid for some bodywork but chose to save the money and use it to cover the cost of finding my sister."

"And what about that little red rosebud tied onto the antenna with the ribbon?"

She crossed her arms and stopped dead in her tracks. "What's wrong with that?"

"Do you forget where you're parked?"

Once in a while, when she had her mind on other things. But she'd be darned if she'd admit it.

The best defense was a good offense, she'd always been told. "You don't think that I've got you figured out, too? What kind of man drives a vintage sports car?"

"One who likes to eat in diners, drink cherry Cokes and listen to oldies on a jukebox."

"Or perhaps one who wants to appear more manly, more powerful? More potent?"

"Yeah, right." He surprised her by opening the passenger door. "Get in." His voice held a rugged, demanding edge, yet his hand gently slid from her back.

The man was a contradiction if she'd ever met one.

As she stooped to climb into the passenger seat, she flashed more of her leg than she'd intended. She glanced up, not at all surprised to see him watching, appreciation glimmering in his eye.

"By the way," she said, "I just figured out another reason you have this car. You like to watch women get in and out of it."

He shot her a crooked grin. "Yep. You've got me pegged, all right."

Something told her that she didn't. Not completely. But there was no doubt about some things. Rico Garcia was a ladies' man. And after his initial gruffness, a real charmer.

If a woman wasn't careful, she could be easily swept off her feet.

Rico closed her door, then walked around the car and slid behind the wheel. As the engine roared to life, Molly decided to hang on to her hat.

And to her better judgment.

## Chapter Three

At a quarter to six Rico and Molly arrived at Antonio's, a waterfront restaurant that offered diners the charm of old-world Italy and a gorgeous view of Lake Lassiter as it sat amidst the rolling lawns of the city park.

When Rico told the hostess they were with the Osterhout party, the young woman led them past a rustic stone fireplace and into a dining room with textured white plaster walls separated by dark wood beams. She escorted them to a linen-draped table near the large bay window that would allow them to watch the sun slide into the pristine water.

Rico held Molly's chair as she took a seat, then sat across from her.

It was one of the most romantic settings she had ever seen, and for a moment it seemed as though she was on a date with the handsome private investigator—as silly as that was. She'd never date a man like Rico, but that didn't mean she was immune to his heart-strumming smile or his musky, mountain-crisp scent.

She was, however, determined to ignore the effect he had on her.

Rico asked the hostess if she'd send over some bread.

"Of course, sir."

When the woman walked away, Rico cast Molly a Casanova smile. "Did I mention being hungry?"

"A couple of times." She couldn't help but grin.

"The dentist will have to forgive me for being rude and not waiting. But I've got to eat something."

"I'm sure he and your mom will understand."

She'd meant to bring up the subject of her sister while they rode in his car, but the timing hadn't seemed right. So they had talked about his Corvette, about the mint condition of the interior, the speed it reached on an open road. The car suited him, she supposed.

Moments later, when one of the busboys brought water and set a basket on the table, Rico offered Molly the first choice of several small precut loaves of fresh-baked bread—French, sourdough, pumpernickel....

She took a slice of the baguette, and he chose the sourdough.

"So," he said, taking his knife and smearing a thick

slab of butter on his bread, "tell me about the sister you want to locate."

Molly wasn't sure where to begin. There were some things she never revealed to the men she ate dinner with. In fact, there were some memories she'd never even shared with her friends.

But this was different. Rico was a private investigator, and she'd tell him anything she could remember that might help him locate Lori.

"I was born in Los Angeles," she began, "the oldest of two girls. My dad was an on-again, off-again junkie, and I don't remember much about my mother other than she left one night to buy a pack of cigarettes and never came back."

Rico listened intently, his demeanor taking on a professional air, which made it easier for her to share the things she kept close to the vest.

"My father was pretty worthless," she admitted, "so I took over as a surrogate mother to my younger sister, Lori."

Rico took a sip of water and watched her over the rim of his glass. He didn't speak, didn't prod her to keep going, but an intensity in his eyes told her he was listening carefully.

"My dad wasn't big on wasting what little money he brought home on groceries, so I'd have to be a little creative." She shrugged. "You know, soda crackers and beer nuts for breakfast, stale-bread-and-ketchup sandwiches for lunch. That sort of thing."

Again she tried to read something in his eyes—sympathy, disgust. Something that might suggest she ought to keep quiet and hold on to the rest of the ugliness. But he merely listened, hiding his opinion as a professional should.

Earlier he'd told her that he'd seen the seedy side of life. She supposed he was realizing that she'd seen a bit of it herself.

She picked up her fork and ran a finger across the edge of the tines, then replaced it beside her plate. For a moment she struggled with making eye contact, then shrugged it off and caught his gaze. "One day when I was eleven, we were left alone for several days, and I had to scavenge around for food…."

His dark brow twitched—the only sign of a response she'd seen so far.

"Not in Dumpsters," she told him, in case his thoughts had gone in that direction. "But there was a little taco shop down the street—Rosarita's. And sometimes the manager would give me some leftover menudo or a couple of bean burritos. There was also a newsstand that sold coffee and sweet rolls to its customers. The guy who worked on weekends, Harold, would give me day-old donuts for free."

"I knew a couple of guys like that."

She wasn't sure what he meant, but for some reason she sensed they'd touched upon a commonality.

"Anyway," she said, "I found this dirty, scraggly dog that afternoon, hanging out at the rear entrance of the

Laundromat. It was hard enough finding food for Lori and I to eat, but I couldn't just let that little guy stay on the street."

The hint of a smile tugged at Rico's lips. "I figured you for an animal lover."

"I don't know about that. I don't have any pets now."

"Why not?"

She shrugged. "Cats and dogs need love and attention, and I'm not home very much. It wouldn't be fair to them. But I'm sure glad I took Petey back to our apartment that day."

"Why?"

"Two days later, in the middle of the night, he started barking like crazy and licking my face. And when I woke up, I smelled smoke."

"Smart dog."

"Petey was definitely a hero. Thanks to him, I managed to get my sister to safety."

"Sounds like you were a hero, too."

His voice had softened, hinting at a tenderness she'd yet to see in him. But she brushed off the hint of sentiment, as well as the compliment, unwilling to take any credit for doing what she'd always done—looking out for herself and her sister. "When the fire department arrived and found Lori and me unsupervised, with no food in the cupboards and the power turned off, they notified the police."

"I hope they nailed your old man for child neglect."

"They did. They also found drug paraphernalia all

over the place." In spite of her desire to be objective and informative in revealing the past, tears stung her eyes. She blinked away the emotion the best she could and continued. "Lori and I were taken to the county receiving home that night and got the first hot meal we'd had in ages."

"Good."

"Yes, it was. But they wouldn't let Petey go with us." She swiped at her eye, catching an escaping tear. "I think he ended up at the pound."

"At least he was better off there than on the streets."

"I hope so." She sucked in a wobbly breath and slowly blew it out. "But I owed that dog something and I've always felt as though I let him down."

"You were a kid. And it was out of your hands."

"I keep telling myself that, but I still feel badly about leaving that sweet little dog behind."

"When did all that happen?" he asked.

"Twelve years ago. I was eleven, and Lori was six." She glanced at the table and swept her hand across the linen, flattening out imaginary wrinkles. "A couple months later the social worker told us that my father had signed the paperwork that released us for adoption."

Rico didn't seem unusually sympathetic—or cynical—which actually made it easier to talk, to pour her heart out.

His professional demeanor shouldn't have surprised her, though. She'd done a little research on the Internet

and learned that Garcia and Associates claimed to be
both elite and discreet. And the firm had been enor-
mously successful. She doubted a company achieved all
that if the owner allowed his emotions to get in the way.

And that was fine with her. She wasn't looking for
sympathy; she was looking for her sister.

"Is that when you and Lori were separated?"

"It happened about six months later. They found a home
for Lori, but the couple who adopted her didn't want two
children, especially one who was almost a teenager."

"What was their name?"

"I don't know. When I asked the social worker if I
could call or send Lori a letter, I was told that it had been
a closed adoption. Her new parents thought she would
be better off starting fresh, forgetting the past."

*Forgetting me.*

Molly's eyes grew misty again, and she cursed the
emotion that welled in her chest. She'd only wanted to
relay the facts that would facilitate his investigation.

She'd never been a crybaby before, and for some
dumb reason, it mattered what Rico thought of her.


Damn. Rico didn't know what to think, what to do.

The story Molly had told him made him angry at her
parents, angry at the system. And it pissed him off that
he couldn't think of anything to say or do to comfort her.

He'd always been uneasy when women cried, which
was a big reason he never let any of his dates or lovers
get close enough to lean on him.

Not that he couldn't sympathize with people.

Hell, he'd had clients that he'd felt sorry for, like good-hearted husbands and wives who'd learned their "loving" spouses had been cheating on them. Or poor Mrs. Chisolm, the grieving widow who'd known nothing about her late husband's business, then had been bilked by an unscrupulous employee she'd trusted.

But this was different. And it was too close to home.

He handed Molly the linen napkin that had been draped across his lap, hoping she'd wipe away the painful memories, as well as her tears.

"Thank you." She took the cloth from him, then blotted her eyes and sniffled. "I'm sorry for falling apart."

"You're allowed." He cleared his throat, wishing he could say something comforting, something witty. When nothing came to mind, he clamped his mouth shut.

"Lori is eighteen now," Molly said. "And no one can stop us from being sisters again. So I need to find her."

"I'll see what I can do."

"Thank you, but I don't expect any favors." She placed the napkin beside her water glass, tucked a strand of hair behind her ear and sat up straight. "I'll pay your fees."

"We can talk about money later. I'll do the initial investigation as a courtesy."

She sniffled again, and he struggled with the urge to reach across the table and take her hand, to offer her more than a napkin.

Before either of them could speak, his cell phone rumbled.

"Excuse me." He glanced at the screen, saw a local number he didn't recognize. "Hello?"

"Honey, it's me."

His mom.

He glanced at the two empty place settings. "Where are you?"

"I'm at Daniel's office. And there's been another emergency. He's on call for another dental group this weekend, and I'm afraid we can't make it to dinner for at least an hour. Please go ahead and order for you and Molly. We'll pick up some fast food, then meet you back at my house. We can have coffee together. In fact, please save room for dessert. I made some of those fudge brownies you like."

Rico looked at Molly, wondering again if this was indeed a matchmaking ploy on his mom's part. But what the hell. They were here now. Just the two of them. And he was starving. "Sure, Mom. I'll talk to you later."

When the line disconnected, he sat back in his seat and looked at his pretty blond companion. "It's only going to be you and me this evening."

Molly arched a delicate brow. "Is it my imagination or do you get the idea that your mom is trying to set us up?"

For a moment he stumbled on which direction to take. After all, he knew better than to get involved with any of his mom's friends or acquaintances, especially since his relationships didn't last very long and he didn't want things to get…sticky for anyone involved.

But Molly didn't seem too head over heels about being with him. And the tone of her voice suggested she was taking this all in stride.

"The same thought crossed my mind," Rico admitted, "but I figured she'd given up on me a couple of years back. I'm not the marrying kind."

"Well, I *am* the marrying kind," Molly said with a smile. "And your mom knows it. I appreciate the gesture, but I don't want to get involved with you. You're not my type."

He wasn't?

Why not?

Not that it mattered. He was just curious, that's all.

Hell, even if he'd go so far as to have a fling with one of his mom's friends, things would really get sticky if Molly was expecting white lace and promises while all he wanted from a relationship was sex.

"So," she said, "I think it's easier if we let her know there's no chemistry between us."

No chemistry?

The hell there wasn't. He'd seen her look at him when she thought he wasn't paying attention, seen her run a nervous tongue across her lips and fiddle with her silverware. He made her nervous, in a sexual way—and he'd lay his last dollar on it.

In spite of having no interest in dating someone like Molly, something tugged at him—chemistry, lust or whatever she wanted to call it.

He didn't want to be conceited, but most women found him attractive. *Very* attractive.

And Molly didn't?

For a moment doubt niggled at his ego.

"So," she said, skipping right over his bruised pride. "Assuming you're going to help me find my sister, how long do you think it will take?"

It took him a moment to recover, to jump right back into the conversation they'd been having before his mom called, to ignore the fact Molly might not find him attractive.

Hell, he knew they were total opposites and a breakup ready to happen. But what did that have to do with sex?

Or attraction.

She leaned forward, her breasts straining against the knit fabric of her dress. "You *do* think we'll find her, don't you?"

Who? Her sister. "Yeah, probably. I'll assign the initial footwork to Cowboy, one of my new associates. He's already in the Los Angeles area working on another case, so he might be able to uncover something."

"Cowboy?" she asked.

God, she had pretty eyes. He'd never seen a pair that green before, that expressive.

"Is that his name?" she asked again. *"Cowboy?"*

"No, it's just a nickname. He's from Texas and has one of those slow Southern drawls. But he's a damn good P.I. and he'll turn up something."

The waiter stopped by to take their dinner order.

Molly chose the angel-hair pasta, Rico asked for the prime rib.

"Thank you for helping me." She cast him a smile that made his stomach wobble and his chest thump.

They didn't talk much after that, just watched the sun set over the lake, listened to the sounds of a baby grand piano playing a romantic concerto in the lounge.

It was hard to ignore the ambience.

Or the beautiful woman seated across from him.

A couple of times, when she looked out the window, he stole a glance at her, studied the way the white-gold strands in her hair glistened in the candlelight.

She turned, caught him staring, and their gazes locked. Something passed between them—that chemistry she said was lacking, he suspected.

He sensed she'd been lying, so why had she said it?

When their meals were served, they each dug into their plates, savoring the taste, the silence—and ignoring the sexual attraction that hovered over the table like a purple elephant with green hummingbird wings.

After they finished eating, the waiter came by to ask if they wanted to see the dessert tray. "The tiramisu is a specialty of the house," he said.

Rico declined for them both, telling Molly, "My mom wants us to save room for coffee and brownies at her house."

"All right."

When the bill arrived, Molly tried to pay, but Rico

refused to even consider it—and not because he was too macho to let a woman treat.

It hadn't started out as a date, but it had kind of evolved into something like that. And even though he'd never take her out again, he wanted to wrap the evening up right.

No need for her to think of him as a jerk. Or as some guy who didn't know how to treat a lady.

He did.

As they walked out of Antonio's, Molly gasped and grabbed his forearm, sending a surge of heat through his bloodstream. "I left my purse inside."

Apparently the woman he suspected would forget where she parked her car at the mall couldn't keep track of her personal belongings either.

He tossed her a smile. "Wait here. I'll get it for you."

"All right. Thanks."

He returned to their table and found her purse hanging by the shoulder strap on the back of her chair, so he picked it up and carried it back outside.

She stood near a rosebush, gazing at a new moon.

The black fabric of her dress hugged her body in a perfect, sexy fit. He was again struck by that damned "no chemistry" comment she'd made earlier, and his ego took another stumble. In spite of his better judgment, the rebel in him flared to life.

"Hey," he said as he sauntered toward her, the purse dangling from his hand.

She turned and smiled. "Thank you."

"You're welcome." He closed the distance between them until they were face-to-face. "I have a bone to pick with you."

Her eyes grew wide. "You do? Why?"

"I don't want you lying to my mom."

"What are you talking about?" Her furrowed brow and the indignant tone of her voice taunted him, tempted him. "I would never lie to her."

He slipped his hand around to the back of her neck, under the silky curtain of her hair. His thumb caressed the softness along her jaw.

Her eyes widened, yet she didn't flinch, didn't push him away. "What are you doing?"

He brushed his lips across hers once, twice.

She sucked in her breath but didn't move. Didn't speak, didn't stop him. Instead she placed a tentative hand on his chest, then slowly gripped the lapel of his jacket—to steady herself, no doubt. Or maybe to draw him closer?

Her lips parted, and he boldly swept his tongue inside, tasting, seeking.

He'd only meant to tease her, to taunt her as she'd been doing to him. But damn. She turned toward him, sliding her arms around his neck, heating up the kiss to a blood-pounding, head-spinning level.

When a car turned in to the parking lot, flashing its headlights at them, Molly finally came to her senses and pulled away. "What in the world was that all about?"

"You're not my type either," he told her. "So tell my mother that I'm rude or a cynical jerk. Tell her I'm a die-hard bachelor who never wants to settle down with one woman. That I'm stubborn and cocky and too damn set in my ways."

She merely stared at him, her lips swollen, a red flush on her cheeks and neck.

"But don't tell her there's no chemistry between us," he added, flashing her a rebel grin.

"Because *that*, sweet Molly, would a be bold-faced lie."

## Chapter Four

Molly's head spun—not just because of the kiss she and Rico had shared but because of the words he'd spoken. The truth he'd forced her to acknowledge.

When she'd said there wasn't any chemistry between them, she'd been lying to him—and to herself. But once their lips touched, their tongues met...

Kaboom.

There'd been no denying the rush of desire. No ignoring her wobbly knees, her racing pulse.

He opened the passenger door for her, and she slid inside the sleek black Corvette.

As he strode around the back of the car, she fingered her lips, touching where his mouth had been.

How could he do that? Kiss her senseless and make her want more? Tease her with a sexy kiss they both knew wasn't going anywhere?

Like a mindless wimp, consumed by passion, she'd kissed him back. Thoroughly. And without any foresight.

Getting romantically involved with Rico would be a mistake. He was all wrong for her.

As he slid behind the wheel and started the high-performance engine, the vintage race car roared to life, and he backed out of the parking space and headed onto the city streets.

She couldn't have forced a comment even if she'd wanted to. Or if she'd actually known what to say.

Fortunately he didn't speak either.

Instead he turned on the radio to a preset jazz station—obviously one of his favorites.

So other than the sounds of Kenny G and later Chuck Mangione, they rode in silence.

And that was just as well. The darn pheromones and hormones that had been frantically hovering overhead while they'd kissed outside the restaurant had followed them into the compact interior. With each breath she took, sexual awareness threatened to explode into something bigger than the both of them.

Rico was a walking, talking heartbreak, especially for a woman who had a carefully planned future in the suburbs with a loving husband and two or three children.

She risked a glance across the console and saw that

he gazed straight ahead, hiding his thoughts, holding his emotions in check. Once they arrived at his mother's house, she hoped she could do as well. She didn't need for things to get…awkward and uncomfortable.

Lori was her first priority, and she couldn't let those crazy, irrational sexual urges take over. Lusting after the P.I. who'd promised to find her sister might ruin everything.

Rico pulled into the driveway and parked on the left, leaving room for Colette to get her car into the garage. He cut the engine but didn't withdraw the keys from the ignition.

Instead, his gaze laid into her, causing her heart to kerplunk, sputter and thud in her ears.

"I'm sorry about kissing you," he said. "That was way out of line."

She merely nodded, afraid her voice wouldn't hold up under the strain of whatever was ricocheting through the air they shared.

"I've never done that before," he admitted.

Involuntarily her brow lifted. Done what? Kissed a woman? Impossible. The guy was an ace.

A dark shank of hair had tumbled onto his forehead, suggesting the kiss had rumpled him a bit, too. One side of his mouth quirked into a smile, implying that he found the whole thing amusing anyway.

She, on the other hand, didn't find anything funny about losing her head and practically making out in public.

"I've never gone to dinner with one of my mother's friends," he explained. "And I damn sure never kissed one of them."

"Don't worry about it," she said, trying to make light of something that would probably haunt her sleep this evening. "I might have downplayed my attraction, but I'm not interested in having that kind of relationship with you."

"That's good." He placed a hand on the gearshift, almost caressing it, and shot her a crooked grin. "I don't make commitments. And I'd hate to have things get…"

"Awkward," she supplied.

"Yeah. And sticky. Especially since you and my mom are friends."

"And because you and I aren't suited for each other," she added.

"That, too." His smile slid over her heart—or rather, her chest. "Now that we have that settled, let's go inside and tear into those brownies. I'm still hungry."

He was? He'd eaten a man-size portion of prime rib, a huge baked potato and all the trimmings, not to mention the ton of bread and butter he'd inhaled.

Of course, like a big kid who didn't give a darn about the things that were good for him, he'd skipped the veggies.

As Rico got out of the car, Molly quickly did the same. It was best if they didn't act as though they'd been on a date. As though there hadn't been a hint of how good it could be between them—assuming they both wanted the same things out of life.

And they definitely didn't.

If there was one thing Molly didn't need, it was a don't-fence-me-in bachelor with a bigger "little black book" than Casanova and Don Juan combined.

Rico hadn't waited for his mom to come home to brew coffee or break out the brownies.

As soon as they got inside the house, he left Molly in the living room and escaped to the kitchen.

If there'd been any question before about the promise of passion that simmered between them, there wasn't anymore. The blood-stirring kiss they'd shared had convinced him they'd be damn good in bed together.

But the reality of their differences was too great to ignore.

Molly was a wedding planner, for Pete's sake. A romantic who, by her own admission, wanted to get married.

And hell, Rico never even *attended* weddings—other than his mother's.

So he'd slipped into a take-it-or-leave-it mode when they'd gotten into the car.

Trouble was, if he had the chance, he'd kiss her again.

But that was a chance he couldn't afford to take. So when she'd asked if she could help in the kitchen, he'd told her no, then whipped up some coffee and cut into the pan of brownies his mom had made. While the hot water trickled through the grounds into the carafe, he ate two of the moist, chocolaty treats.

He bypassed his mom's fancy china cups, opting for a couple of the mugs he'd given her last year. Coffee was made to be savored hot, black and rich. And it was made to be served in sturdy mugs rather than itty-bitty, paper-thin teacups.

"Hey, Molly," he called toward the living room where he'd left her. "How do you like your coffee?"

"With cream and sugar."

That didn't surprise him. He figured her for a light-weight, especially when it came to jolts of caffeine. Or most everything else, he suspected.

A woman like her needed a man to look after her. And Rico wasn't up for the job—no matter how pretty she was, how sweet her kisses.

He carried a tray into the living room, where he found her studying the photographs displayed on the man-tel—pictures of his mom and Frank when they honey-mooned in Maui, Rico in his police uniform the day he graduated from the academy. That sort of thing.

She looked up when he entered and lifted a silver-framed photograph of him in a Little League uniform. "Is this you?"

"Yeah."

It had been taken the day he'd hit a game-winning grand slam.

"You were a cute kid," she said.

"Thanks."

Her smile caught him off guard—or maybe it was the way her eyes glimmered that made his steps slow, his pulse kick up a notch.

"I don't have any pictures of me and Lori as kids. There were a couple of school pictures, but…well, I'm sure they were destroyed in the fire. Either way, once we were taken to Hilldale Receiving Home, we never went back to the apartment. And what little we had was lost."

His heart went out to her, but he tried to rein it in. Something told him she wasn't asking for sympathy, but it still made him sad that her childhood had been a lot worse than his.

The words slipped out anyway. "I'm sorry that your early years were so crappy."

"They were. But the later years made up for them. I had the best foster parents in the world."

"Your optimism is a bit surprising," he said, "under the circumstances."

She shrugged. "I choose to be content rather than bitter. To trust rather than doubt."

So did his mother. But Rico had never seen the wisdom in having a philosophy like that.

She replaced the photograph, then strode toward him, tucking a strand of hair behind her ear, revealing the gentle curve of her jaw.

His arms grew antsy, itching to wrap around her and draw her near. But he knew better than to let her get too close. The fire in their kiss had been temptation of the worst kind and a real wake-up call to keep his hands and his mouth to himself.

So he decided to let the subject drop.

They each took a mug, then sat. This time he took the easy chair, leaving the sofa for her. But for some reason, the conversation stalled.

He hated the silence, the awkwardness.

The memory of the kiss that continued to hover over them.

Rather than chance a discussion about attraction and chemistry, he set down his coffee. "You know, I'm going to need all the information you can give me about your family—full names, birthdates, that kind of thing."

"I'll tell you everything I can remember."

Good. A new focus.

He opened the drawer of the light oak end table, where his mom kept a notepad and pen.

"My last name is really Grimes," Molly said, "but ever since high school I've been going by Townsend."

"Why?"

"The Townsends were my foster parents, although they became much more than that." She glanced down at the mug she held with both hands. "I always planned to legally change my name, although for some reason I didn't. And I figure I'll eventually get married and I'd have to change it again…."

Whoa. He didn't need to go there. "How about your biological parents? What were their names?"

"David and Tina Grimes, although I'm not sure my mom and dad ever got married."

"I'll need birthdates, too," he told her.

"Mine is February 2, 1982. Lori was born five years later, on May 7."

He asked where they'd been born, where they last lived, the name of the county facility where they'd been placed. And she supplied him answers.

"I'll also need to know the name of your social worker."

"First there was Fran Davies, followed by Ralph Sanchez," she said.

"Who handled the adoption?"

"I don't know. Fran wouldn't tell me. She said it was closed."

He nodded, then asked about the fire, the apartment complex, the street on which they'd lived.

Molly gave him as much information as she could.

"What was the name of that taco shop?

She paused, her brow furrowed. "Rosarita's. How will that help?"

"You never know." His pen scratched across the page as he wrote out her answer.

"I'm not sure that the newsstand had a name, but Harold was the guy I used to talk to. He was about fifty, I think. Heavyset, with thick eyebrows and one of those mustaches that twirled on both sides."

Rico nodded, making notes, asking more questions. And when he thought he'd had enough—or rather, when he heard the sound of an approaching vehicle and realized his mom and her boyfriend had arrived and the heat was off for a while—he set down the notepad and settled back into the overstuffed cushions.

Thank goodness.

When the doorknob turned, he stood, expecting to meet his mom's fiancé and preparing to shake hands and give the new step-dentist a face-to-face assessment. But his mom entered alone.

She smiled, but her eyes—red, puffy and a little misty—told another story.

Where the hell was the dentist?

And what had he done to make her cry?

"Are you okay?" Rico asked.

"Yes, I'm fine. Just a little disappointed, since I've been so eager to have you and Daniel meet. But something else came up, and he can't come by this evening." Another smile broke free, but Rico suspected it had been a struggle for her.

But hey, maybe this was the start of a breakup.

Not that Rico wanted to see his mom hurt, but better now than later. And sometimes the answer to prayer arrived on the tail of what appeared to be bad news. At least, when Rico had been a kid and been desperate enough to talk to The Man Upstairs, that's how it had seemed to work.

"Daniel will be here for breakfast," his mom said, her voice trying to rally.

"Another emergency?" Molly asked.

"Yes, but not a patient. Daniel received a call through his answering service, one he had to return in private. A business issue he couldn't discuss in front of me. Something that might take a while."

Rico's radar kicked in. Not that he was an expert on relationships, but if a guy was going to marry a woman, weren't they supposed to be up front with each other?

So what was the big deal, the big secret?

He hadn't liked the idea of his mom getting married again, and this didn't make him feel any better about it. Not when it came to trusting a guy who didn't want to talk to her about a business issue. If that's what it really was.

Damn. This was a Saturday night. Maybe the good dentist was trying to juggle two lovers.

"Well, I don't suppose there's any reason for me to stick around," Molly said, "if we're not going to discuss the wedding."

She was right, Rico thought. And if their luck held, there might not be a wedding after all.

Yet for some unexplained reason, he wasn't in any hurry to see Molly rush out the door.

"I'm sorry we didn't get to have dinner together this evening," his mom told her pretty, young friend. "But please come by for breakfast tomorrow. Daniel will be here. And I'd really like you here when we discuss the wedding plans."

"All right."

They agreed on nine o'clock.

As Molly stood and reached for her purse, Rico fought the urge to stand, to follow her outside. To talk to her about the kiss. To see if he could finagle another one.

And how foolish was that?

Instead his mom followed Molly to the door, then stepped outside with her.

Girl talk, he suspected. They were friends, after all. At least, that's what they'd both told him.

He just hoped his name didn't come up. Or the fact that he'd kissed the wedding planner. His mom wouldn't need ammo like that.

Because if she thought there was an outside chance that Rico and Molly might hit if off, she'd really start to meddle.

"So what do you think?" Collette asked Molly as they stepped outside and headed toward Molly's car.

"About what?"

"About Rico."

Molly's heart thudded in her chest until it reverberated in her ears and triggered a flood of warmth in her cheeks. "He's very nice. And I appreciate his offer to help me find my sister."

"He's handsome, don't you think?"

"Yes, he is."

"Is there any…you know, attraction going on between you?"

Molly's initial reaction was to deny it, to fall back on the no-chemistry line she'd been planning to use. But the kiss that had nearly knocked her to her knees, along with Rico telling her not to lie to his mother, stirred her conscience to an honorable level. "Yes, Colette, there is. We're both attracted to each other. But we also realize that dating would be a mistake. We want different things out of life."

"That's really not true," the older woman said. "Rico needs a woman like you, needs to settle down and get married. To have children. He just doesn't know it yet."

What was Molly supposed to say to a maternal misconception like that?

Even in the one evening Molly had known him, Rico made it clear that he wasn't the marrying kind. And she suspected he was perfectly happy with his no-strings philosophy when it came to romance—whether his mother thought so or not.

Molly placed an arm around Colette. "I know how badly you'd like to have grandchildren. And finding Rico a wife is the first step. But if and when he decides to get married, it won't be to me."

"Are you sure?" Colette asked, her voice unwilling to give up its hold on hope.

"Very sure." Molly gave her a quick squeeze. "I have

certain qualities I'm looking for in a man. And your son, as gorgeous as he is, doesn't have many of them."

Colette clucked her tongue and blew out a sigh. "Is that all that's holding you back? A list you came up with?"

Pretty much. That and the fact Rico seemed a lot like a player.

"I'm very particular about certain things."

"And you should be. But I just hope you have sexual compatibility as a high priority."

Actually that was at the bottom of Molly's list. Some things were more important than sex. But she didn't want to discuss that with Colette. Not when the heated memory of that darn kiss urged her to bump sex up to a higher level of priority.

As she reached into her purse and pulled out her car keys, she glanced at the Corvette parked in the driveway.

"You know," she said to Colette, "I probably should have asked Rico, but I wondered why he drives a vintage car rather than a new model with all the extras."

Colette grinned, the edges of her eyes crinkling with the warmth of her smile. "I knew you didn't have my son figured out."

"What do you mean?"

"That car once belonged to Frank, my second husband. It was his pride and joy. And after he was killed in that hunting accident, we had to sell the vehicle to make ends meet. A couple of years ago, Rico managed to track it down and purchased it for more than it was worth. Then he had it restored to mint condition."

Colette was right. Molly hadn't quite pegged Rico as sentimental, if chasing down his stepfather's car could be considered as such. Of course, that didn't mean she'd changed her mind about dating him.

Hoping to turn the conversation toward a couple who were better suited, Molly asked, "So what's going on with Daniel?"

"Well, he does a lot of consulting on the side. And a call came in from an attorney in Albany. It wasn't something he felt comfortable discussing with me."

When Molly fell in love with the man of her dreams, she didn't want any secrets between them. "Are you okay with that?"

Colette shrugged. "I suppose I'll have to be. If Daniel and I were already married, it wouldn't be an issue. He could just go into his home office and talk privately."

Molly glanced over her shoulder at the living room window, where the muted lamplight peered through a gap in one of the panels of the drawn curtains. "Rico isn't too happy about your marriage."

"I know, but he'll be all right with it as soon as he meets Daniel." Colette sighed. "But just in case, can you try and get him to understand why a wedding is important to us?"

"Sure." At least, Molly would try. Rico wasn't going to be easy to convince. But either way, she would make sure everything was picture-book perfect, from the hydrangeas that would adorn the altar to the limousine that would take Colette and Dr. Osterhout to the airport for the honeymoon trip to Germany.

Colette wrapped her arms around Molly and gave her a gardenia-laced hug. "If I would have had a daughter, I would have wanted her to be you."

Molly blinked back a tear. "Thank you."

If wishes were magic, she would have loved to have had Colette as her mother, too. She glanced again at the curtains, at the light shining from within the house. But that would have made Rico her brother.

And then he'd really be off-limits.

She thought she caught a glimpse of his silhouette, a shadow of his form. Tall, buff. And far more attractive than a man should be.

He was probably wolfing down brownies, completely oblivious to Molly's thoughts.

The kiss had probably faded from his memory hours ago. And that was just as well.

So why did she hope that it hadn't?

## Chapter Five

Rico fought the urge to peer outside, to see if Molly and his mom were talking, to figure out whether he was the topic of their discussion.

But how adolescent was that?

Instead he grabbed the telephone from the lamp table and dialed Cowboy's cell number.

The tall, lanky Texan answered on the third ring.

"Hey, it's me," Rico said. "How's it going?"

"Fine as frog's hair," drawled Trenton James Whittaker, otherwise known as Cowboy. "I'm planning to hit some of the L.A. clubs tonight."

Cowboy not only worked hard but he played hard. And the fact that he was going out on the town told Rico his job was through. "How'd your case wrap up?"

"Mrs. Summerville is going to be pleased with the pretty pictures I took. 'Course, her husband is going to be in a hell of a fix."

Anita Summerville was a lovely fifty-year-old woman who suspected that her husband of twenty-seven years was cheating on her. And she'd been right. Rico never liked to be the one to break news like that to ladies like her. But then again, that's what she was paying Garcia and Associates to uncover.

"Can you stick around in southern California for a couple of days?" Rico asked. "I've got another job for you."

"Sure thing, boss. What's up?"

"It's just a side job. I'm doing a favor for a friend of my mom's. She wants us to locate her sister, an eighteen-year-old young woman who was adopted twelve years ago."

Cowboy didn't respond right away. "Sounds like your mom is hobnobbing with some mighty young friends."

"Yeah, well, my mom travels to the beat of her own golden-oldie band." Rico raked a hand through his hair and glanced at the door his mother still had yet to open and enter.

He supposed this could wait, but the sooner he located Molly's sister, the sooner he could be rid of Molly herself.

Or rather, the sooner he would be rid of the lust she aroused and the sooner he could put a stop to his mother's misguided attempts to orchestrate a romance or—God forbid—a double wedding.

Damn. Just the thought of a formal commitment made him—a guy his employees considered unshakeable—break out in a cold sweat.

Rico could, of course, easily imagine Molly in a white, floor-length bridal gown, smiling as pretty as you please. It was the thought of himself standing beside her in a tuxedo that made him want to run like hell.

Those penguin suits were too constraining, too uncomfortable for a guy like him. And so was what they represented.

"Should I grab a pen and paper?" Cowboy asked.

"Yeah." Rico reached for the notepad he'd left on the coffee table.

"All right, boss. Shoot."

Rico repeated the information Molly had given him. When he finished, he added, "It was a closed adoption, so start by trying to find her old man. He was arrested about twelve years ago on drug charges. And probably for child neglect, if not flat-out abuse."

"Sounds like he's a real piece of work."

"Yeah." Rico raked a hand through his hair. "If you can't find anything through the normal channels, you might ask some questions in their old neighborhood on the south side of Lakeridge. There has to be someone still around who remembers that apartment fire, as well as David Grimes. We need to find the guy. Lori couldn't have been adopted without his signature. And he may know something about her new parents."

"I'll get on it in the morning," Cowboy said. "And I'll let you know when I get a lead."

As the call ended, the front door swung open and Rico's mom stepped inside.

"So what do you think?" she asked him.

"About what?"

She shot him a dreamy-eyed, hundred-watt smile. "About Molly, of course. Isn't she pretty?"

Molly was a knockout. But Rico knew better than to admit that to his mother. If she knew he had the hots for her young friend, she'd slip into yenta mode in the blink of an eye.

"She's okay," he admitted.

His mom arched an auburn brow and crossed her arms. "Come on, Rico. She's better than 'okay.' She's absolutely beautiful. *And,* on top of that, she's a blonde."

He gave her a so-what shrug, hoping to fend off any more of her questions yet knowing it wasn't likely to work.

She clucked her tongue. "When I tried to set you up with Angela Waterbury, you told me you didn't like brunettes. And when I introduced you to Donna Hulett, you told me you weren't into redheads. So that leaves the blondes, which I began to realize were all you dated in high school. And so I've had a dickens of a time finding one you might be attracted to while making sure she was wife-and-mother material."

"I've told you before. I'm not going to settle down and get married. Not for a long time—*if ever.*" He cast a glance at his mother, wondering how she was taking the cold, hard facts.

But dang, she was resilient. Her smile never skipped a beat. She sat on the sofa and plopped both hands on her knees. "Molly's sweet, don't you think?"

He wasn't going to lie. Not to his mom. "Yes, she is." Sugarplum-fairy sweet. White-lace-and-spring-bouquet sweet.

"By the way," his mom said, her smile turning smug, "Molly admitted to the chemistry between you."

She did?

In spite of wanting to downplay it all, his ego soared and a grin tickled his lips.

So the kiss and his speech about honesty had worked. Not that he'd actually expected her to admit anything to his mother. *He* wouldn't have.

"So," his mom said, "are you going to admit the attraction, too?"

Rico's impulse was to deny it, even though that would make him a liar in his mom's eyes—and a hypocrite in Molly's. But hell, why change tactics now? He was always up front with the women in his life, whether it was his mother or the ones who were just passing through. And that's just what Molly would be. Another attractive woman he'd flirted with and would send on her way.

"What do you want me to admit?" he asked. "That your pretty blond friend is a hell of a kisser?"

His mother's mouth dropped and her eyes widened. "You kissed her?"

Apparently Molly hadn't been as forthright as she could have been.

"Sure. We kissed."

"And it was good?"

Rico gave a little shrug, wishing he hadn't brought it up but unwilling to backpedal. "Yeah. It was good." Damn good. "But you'd better back off, Mom—if you value your friendship with the bridal consultant."

"Why's that?"

"Because I'd be open to sex but nothing more. And Molly's the kind of woman who'd be hurt if she agreed to that kind of a relationship with me."

"You wouldn't hurt Molly," his mother said.

No, he wouldn't. Not on purpose. And that's why he wouldn't agree to take her out on a real date—especially after a kiss that had been a prelude to foreplay and a head-spinning, eye-opening indication of how good they'd be in bed.

But Rico wouldn't sleep with his mother's friend, no matter how blond she was, how pretty. How sweet the memory of their kiss.

Or how appealing the thought of a repeat performance.

\* \* \*

Molly, who prided herself on keeping appointments and being prompt, arrived at Colette's house at ten after nine. But there was a good reason for that. She'd left her headlights on after getting home last night—her battery was dead this morning and she'd had to ask her neighbor for a jump start.

Okay, so she hadn't been thinking clearly, not after that kiss. And certainly not after admitting to Colette—Mr. Wrong's mother, of all people!—her attraction to Rico.

She reached across the console and took her day planner, legal-size notepad and purse from the passenger seat. As she climbed from her car, she scanned the quiet street.

Even with all the trouble she'd had getting here this morning, she'd still managed to beat Dr. Osterhout. His white Cadillac was nowhere to be seen.

She made her way up the sidewalk to the front porch and rang the bell.

When Rico opened the door, wearing a black T-shirt, a pair of jeans and a fresh-from-the-shower smile, her heart nearly catapulted out of her chest.

How could he look even better in the morning than he had from across a candlelit table?

The hint of musk and soap taunted her, as did the memory of that darn kiss. But she managed to squeak out a "Hi" and add, "You…surprised me. I expected your mom to get the door."

"Yeah. Well, I was expecting the dentist. What's with this guy? I'm beginning to think he's a myth, if not a king-size jerk."

Molly wasn't sure what was going on, but she knew there had to be a reasonable explanation. "I'm sure the doctor will be here soon. And when he does, I have no doubt you'll like him as much as I do."

Rico didn't appear to be convinced as he stepped aside and let her in.

"My mom's in the kitchen," he said, closing the door behind her.

As Molly entered the living room, she caught the aroma of fresh-brewed coffee, the warm smell of home-made biscuits baking in the oven and the spicy scent of sausage as it sizzled in a frying pan. She hadn't real-ized how hungry she was until her stomach growled in anticipation.

Colette had been busy and was undoubtedly outdo-ing herself as a cook and hostess.

Rico led Molly past the dining room and through the small doorway that led to the kitchen, where his mother stood over the stove preparing a thick, country-style gravy.

"Good morning," Colette said, bright-eyed, chipper and obviously in her element.

"Is there anything I can do to help?" Molly asked.

"Not a thing." Colette smiled, blue eyes glistening. "Daniel should be here any minute. Why don't you two go sit on the deck. I thought it would be nice to eat outdoors this morning. Spring has really sprung! It's going to be a beautiful day."

Rico started toward the sliding door that led to the patio, and Colette stopped him. "Just a minute. Take this with you."

They waited as she filled a white insulated carafe with fresh-brewed coffee. She handed it to Rico, and he carried it outside.

The table had been beautifully set with pale green woven place mats and matching linen napkins. A vase of daisies made a perfect centerpiece and sat next to a crystal pitcher that held orange juice—fresh-squeezed, most likely. A crystal creamer and sugar bowl, a cube of butter and salt and pepper shakers suggested Colette had everything under control, just as she'd said.

And their hostess had been right about something else. It was a lovely morning. Not too cool, not too warm. A great start to what Molly hoped would be a perfect—and productive—day.

Rico held a chair for her, a polite gesture she tried not to read into. It would be strictly business this morning. They'd finalize the wedding plans, then Molly would be on her way.

She sat, adjusting the hem of her pale yellow sundress as she did so. "Thank you."

"You're welcome." Rico took a seat to the side of her, allowing her the full view of Colette's small but park-like yard, with a lush lawn, a rose garden and a patch of daffodils growing near an old-fashioned wishing well.

Birds chirped from the maple tree, and a dog barked in the distance.

Eating outdoors was a good idea, Molly decided as she hung the strap of her purse over the back of the chair and then placed her notepad and the day planner on the table beside her.

"You know," Rico said, "if the groom fails to show up, we might not have any need for a bridal consultant."

"He'll show up. And there *will be* a beautiful wedding."

He chuffed, and she realized he wasn't just dragging his feet about his mother's upcoming nuptials. She suspected he was actually hoping for a broken engagement—something that would crush his mother *and* the dentist who loved her.

It wasn't easy dealing with a cynic—ever. And it was even more difficult when she couldn't keep her gaze from wandering to his profile, from studying the way his hair curled up at the collar in a not-so-long style that she liked.

As though knowing he'd caught her eye, the handsome P.I. shot her a rebellious smile that turned her heart on end.

And what was with that?

He was *so* not her type, not the kind of man she wanted in her future.

A guy like Rico would fight his bride-to-be every step of the way, from planning the wedding to all the day-to-day compromises needed in a happy marriage.

"How long have you worked at the bridal boutique?" he asked.

"About two years. And it's a perfect job for me. I love it."

"I'm not surprised. You seem like the kind of woman who would get a charge out of sending a couple off in a rain of white rice and empty promises."

Molly stiffened. Rico's pessimism struck an off-key chord in her chest, especially when it came to sacred vows and committed relationships. And she found it aggravating that he'd belittle the optimism she'd fought long and hard to embrace.

But it wasn't worth the fight. Not when she knew she wouldn't come out on top, at least when it came to convincing him to see things her way.

She would, however, set him straight on the rice. "They don't do that anymore."

"They don't do what?"

"Throw rice at the bride and groom. They use birdseed now."

"Birdseed?" He grimaced, causing an interesting crease in his brow. "What the hell is that supposed to symbolize?"

"It doesn't symbolize anything. The birds used to fill up on the rice and then it would swell in their little tummies, causing them to die."

"I guess after a wedding a bunch of dead songbirds would be bad omen, huh? And bad publicity for the wedding planner, too. It would make it tough to peddle your wares and your sunshine-and-lollipop philosophy."

Molly fiddled with the edge of the linen napkin that rested in front of her, trying to remain cool and collected, when she wanted to jump up and down and scream. As much as she strove to remain optimistic, she also struggled with a bit of a temper that she usually managed to rein in.

And let's face it—Rico Garcia could make a mellow, mild-mannered preacher spit and cuss in frustration.

But Molly was a professional, for goodness sake. Able to handle all the personalities that made up the various wedding parties she'd had to orchestrate.

In the past two years she'd dealt with her share of bridezillas, spoiled and nasty brides whose primary focus was on themselves and the attention they'd get rather than the groom or anyone else involved in the special day.

And she'd dealt with deadbeat dads, feuding family members, a drunken justice of the peace, a stray dog that ran off with a bridal bouquet. Why, she'd managed to handle a ton of potential crises.

But she feared she'd met her match with this cynical son of the bride.

"So what's the matter?" he asked her. "Cat got your tongue?"

"No, you've got my goat."

He laughed. "I haven't heard that phrase in a while."

She shrugged, feeling as though she ought to dump

the pitcher of orange juice over his head. Instead she cast him one of her most professional, unflappable smiles. "Am I going to have to fight your negativity every step of the way?"

"Probably." He slid her another rebel grin, and her pulse took off on a rebellious course of its own.

Lordy, Rico would turn her carefully planned, predictable life upside down in a New York minute—if she'd let him.

Rico couldn't help but laugh. The look on Molly's face was priceless. "Maybe we ought to call a truce."

Molly raised her eyebrows. "You mean it?"

Yes and no. He really didn't want to spar with Molly. Maybe because he sympathized with the child she'd been, the woman she'd become. Hell, he didn't know.

His hand lifted of its own accord, and he brushed his knuckles along her cheek, felt the softness, heard her breath catch in the faintest whisper.

A shiver of heat skimmed his bloodstream.

And as her lips parted, he had half a notion to kiss her again—just for the hell of it. At least, that's the reason he'd given himself.

Warning bells sounded in his head, reminding him not to let his hormones take over. A woman like Molly would drive him to an early grave.

He withdrew his hand slowly, unsure of a better way to rewind his touch.

When her emotion-laden gaze locked on to his, quizzing him, accusing him, making him want to run scared, he tried to shrug it off.

But it didn't work.

Inside, the telephone rang, cutting the tension just a tad.

He picked up the carafe. "Coffee?"

"Yes, please."

After filling her cup—one of his mom's delicate pieces of china—he poured his own, wishing he'd brought out a sturdy mug. As a kid, he'd broken several of his mom's good dishes. She'd always told him it was all right, but he'd seen the disappointment on her face, sensed how badly she'd felt about losing something special, something she valued.

Moments later his mother walked outside, tears welling in her eyes. "I'm afraid Daniel has to drive to Albany today and can't make it for breakfast. He wanted me to tell you how badly he feels about this, but he has to testify in court on Monday morning, and the lawyers need to meet with him."

"What's that all about?" Rico asked.

"He's not free to discuss it with me," his mother responded.

Unable?

Or unwilling?

What in the hell kind of trouble had the guy gotten into? And what kind of secrets was he keeping?

The fact that his mom had set herself up for another heartbreak twisted a knot in his gut.

"I knew that guy would prove to be a flake," Rico muttered, "just like the last two guys you hooked up with."

The tears that had been brimming in his mom's eyes began to trickle down her cheeks, and for a moment he regretted speaking his piece. But the dentist was going to hurt her, and the sooner she faced reality, the better.

His mother sniffled and swiped at her tears.

The knot in Rico's gut intensified, making him feel like one of those damned songbirds Molly had talked about, the ones that unwittingly oinked out on dry rice and blew up while the bride and groom rode off into the sunset toward marital discord.

Damn. He didn't want to see his mom cry any more than he wanted to stand by and watch her get hurt.

But right now it was his words that had unleashed her tears.

Realizing that her "soul mate" was a jerk was something she'd have to come up with on her own. Rico would merely have to be around to pick up the pieces, as he had in the past.

"I'm sorry, Mom. That was out of line." He stood and offered her a hug.

"Daniel's not like the others," his mom said, enveloping him in her soft gardenia scent. "You'll see."

Rico chose to accept, at least on the outside, her head-in-the-clouds belief. "I hope so."

"I'm sure there's an explanation," Molly added.

Yeah, like the dental Prince Charming had committed some damn crime upstate. Or that he had another lover or two he was trying to juggle.

But truthfully Rico hoped his mom's boyfriend would prove him wrong.

His cynical nature wasn't buying it, though. So that's why he was going to call his Manhattan office late in the morning and tell Margie he was going to take some time off for personal reasons. And that's why he was going to stick around Westlake long enough to get to the bottom of the dentist's secret life.

He glanced at Molly, saw the emotion bubbling up in her eyes.

Oh, for Pete's sake. He hated it when women cried. It set him on end. Unbalanced him. Made him feel helpless.

And God knew he thrived on being right, on being on top. In control.

"Let's have breakfast while it's hot," his mom said. Then she excused herself and went into the kitchen.

Rico took a seat, yet his gaze wandered to that of the bridal cheerleader. The pretty blonde who was every bit as starry-eyed and unrealistic as his mother was.

She cast him a go-fight-win smile that shouted out her appreciation, her faith. "About the time I wrote you off as coldhearted and unfeeling, you proved me wrong."

"It's early yet."

Lord knew there was plenty of time before a June wedding for him to prove her right, whether he intended to or not.

## *Chapter Six*

The next evening Dr. Osterhout had called Rico's mother and apologized again for having to leave town. His testimony had been given and he was heading home.

He'd promised to make it up to her. And to her son, who he'd been "dying" to meet.

When she'd relayed her boyfriend's message, Rico had nodded as though understanding. Ever since breakfast on Sunday morning he'd been stepping on eggshells when it came to his mother's relationship. He didn't want to be the one to cause her tears.

But he couldn't hold his tongue or sit on his hands forever—even if he had the time off from work to do it.

So although it was Tuesday and they were all supposed to meet that evening, Rico insisted upon driving his mother to Dr. Osterhout's office just before lunch.

If the mountain wouldn't go to the P.I.…

He parked in front of a small white clapboard house on Second Avenue that had been converted to a dental office.

"I know you're still a bit skeptical about Daniel," his mom said.

A bit? Rico clamped his mouth shut, making every effort not to pop off with a sarcastic response.

"But you'll see," she continued. "Daniel isn't just a wonderful man, he's a brilliant doctor. And his patients and staff adore him."

"That's great." Rico climbed from the car. "I'm glad to hear it."

Of course, what he didn't tell her was that it would take more than a couple of character witnesses to convince him the dentist was on the up-and-up.

As they entered what was once a living room and was now a dental waiting room, the receptionist, a matronly brunette, looked up from her work with a smile. "Hi, Colette. The doctor will be glad to know you stopped by. He had us reschedule some of his patients this afternoon so he can leave early and spend some time with you and your son."

The woman's gaze traveled to Rico and her smile intensified. "This must be him."

"It certainly is." Colette beamed as she made the introductions, saying Belinda Carmichael had worked for Daniel ever since he'd opened his practice in Westlake.

"When was that?" Rico asked.

"Nearly four years ago," Belinda said. "If you'll have a seat, I'll let the doctor know you're here."

Not quite four years, huh?

It took a while for a dentist to establish a practice, Rico realized. So why had Osterhout relocated in Westlake?

The questions that demanded answers merely grew in number.

He glanced at his mom, who sat grinning from ear to ear, waiting patiently for her dental dream come true to enter the room.

A disparaging comment came to mind, but Rico held it back and reached for a *Field and Stream* instead.

His mom was a slow learner when it came to character assessment, but they'd all be better off if Dr. Osterhout showed his true colors and she was able to figure it out on her own. Then Rico could help her pick up the pieces of her broken heart as he'd done in the past.

"Colette," a man's jovial voice rang out. "What a wonderful surprise. You're just in time for lunch."

Rico looked up to see a rather nondescript, balding man in his fifties enter from the back office. The dentist, he presumed, if the light blue oversize medical shirt was any indication.

His mom stood, and the smiling doctor gave her an affectionate hug.

Rico got to his feet, too, ready for the customary greeting as soon as the embrace had ended.

When it did, Dr. Osterhout reached out his right arm toward Rico. "I'm so sorry about the canceled dinner plans on Saturday night, as well as breakfast on Sunday."

While they shook hands, Rico noticed the man had a steady grip, solid but not one of those knuckle-crunching attempts to prove his power or his manhood.

Rico still wasn't convinced of the guy's sincerity, though. Or of his innocence. But he shook off his concern for now and managed to utter, "No problem, Doc."

"Listen," Daniel said, flashing a pearly-white smile at the two of them. "I'll be finished here in about fifteen minutes. Why don't we meet at Katrina's Kitchen? It's a little café only a block or two away and an easy walk."

"That sounds lovely," his mom said as she turned to Rico. "Doesn't it?"

Rico gave a half shrug meant to imply *Sure. Whatever.*

He was going to need more than a casual greeting to figure out what kind of guy his mom had pinned her heart on this time.

"Great," the dentist said. "I'll meet you there."

Twenty minutes later Daniel Osterhout joined them in a corner booth at the mom-and-pop-style restaurant known for its home-cooked meals and reasonable prices.

Rico ordered a French dip sandwich with fries. His

mom chose something called the Protein Platter, and the dentist requested a turkey sandwich, a cup of soup and fruit.

Okay, so Osterhout appeared to be health-conscious. Rico, a junk-food addict, wasn't going to hold that against him. But there'd be other hints and clues about his past, his character.

They made the usual small talk over lunch, while Rico tried his damnedest to hold back an out-and-out interrogation until he could talk to the dentist in private. And he wasn't sure when that would happen.

But when Rico's mom excused herself to go to the ladies' room, he got his chance.

"My mother said you had to testify in a court case in Albany." Rico popped a fry in his mouth, trying to remain low-key and casual rather than ready to pounce on the doctor's whereabouts.

Osterhout reached for his glass of water and took a sip, prolonging the answer to Rico's first question. "Yes, I did have to drive to Albany for my testimony."

"Mind if I ask what that was about?"

"No, not if you'll refrain from telling Colette about it."

Rico tensed. Was the guy actually thinking Rico would keep their chat confidential? Of course, unless he agreed not to repeat the secret to his mother, he wouldn't know what the guy had gotten himself involved in. "Sure. I'll keep quiet."

"Do you remember hearing about the Tolliver case?"

Russell Tolliver? Rico wondered, his ears perking up, his interest sufficiently piqued. "You mean the guy who was convicted of the Cedar Valley murders?"

"Yes, that's the one."

About ten years ago, while Rico still worked with the NYPD, Tolliver, a university mail room clerk, had been charged with the brutal slaying of nearly a dozen young college girls. And it had been a forensic dentist who'd managed to identify the victims, as well as link Tolliver to the murders through a signature bite mark on the women's skin.

Had Osterhout been the dentist involved in that case?

"Tolliver is appealing his conviction," Daniel said. "And since I had originally worked on the case, I was called back for the appeal. I expected to testify later this week, but due to a legal technicality that forced the D.A.'s hand, they needed me to come in on Monday."

A bit dumbfounded, Rico didn't immediately respond. It had been an unusually gruesome case. And one that had been highly publicized.

"You've done some forensic dentistry?" Rico asked, still a bit surprised.

"It was my specialty for nearly twenty years."

But now he was in private practice?

"Why'd you give it up?" Rico asked.

"Mary, my wife, used to complain at length about my chosen profession, about the effect she claimed it had on our home life. I tried my best to leave my work at the office, but she insisted it was more than that. It was my attitude, the darkness that dogged me sometimes. And she claimed that some of the cases, especially those that were unsolved, had put a damper on what she called my fun-loving personality."

"Your wife?" Rico asked.

"My late wife. I lost her four years ago, right after she and I moved here and bought out Dr. Ryan's practice."

Rico nodded, as though it all made sense, then realized he ought to say something. "I'm sorry."

Now it was the dentist's turn to nod.

Rico reached for another fry, dipping it into the au jus before eating it. He wasn't sure if he would have given up his career just because a woman wanted him to.

"So you gave it all up?" he asked.

"Yes. My wife and my marriage meant the world to me. So I took some refresher courses at my alma mater and began practicing in Westlake."

"So that's why you didn't share the reason you had to testify yesterday."

The dentist nodded. "I wanted to spare Colette any worries, any concerns."

That made sense. Rico had been trying to spare his mom a lot of things over the years.

"I loved my first wife," Daniel said. "Mary was a wonderful woman. And I never thought I'd find anyone like her again—until I met your mother."

Rico hoped he was telling the truth, but the jury was

still out on Dr. Osterhout. At least until Rico could double-check his story about being the forensic dentist on that Tolliver case.

As his mother walked out of the ladies' room and returned to their booth, she blessed them with a warm smile. "Did I miss anything?"

"No. Not at all." Dr. Osterhout stood to allow Colette to slide into her seat and stole a glance at Rico.

"You didn't miss a thing," Rico added. "We were just having a little man talk and getting to know each other."

"I'm so glad," she said. "Especially since you'll soon be related."

Rico didn't know about that.

But he was feeling a little better about the man his mom wanted to marry, even if a full-on wedding with all the trimmings still didn't sit well with him.

At one-fifteen Susan Sullivan, a twenty-three-year-old socialite who'd become a regular on the Westlake society page of the newspaper, entered Betty's Bridal Boutique with her red-haired maid of honor.

She'd come for a fitting of a Vera Wang original gown she would wear to her well-publicized wedding at the end of June.

The bubbly blonde had taken more time than the norm to decide upon a dress. Of course, the Vera Wang had been her first choice, but her father, while wanting the wedding of the year to be spectacular, had balked at paying more than ten thousand dollars for a gown his daughter would only wear once. But after Susan had changed her mind time and again, making her parents and Molly half-crazy, she'd finally settled on one—the Vera Wang.

And thank goodness her battle-weary father had finally agreed. Not that Molly actually cared either way. But the wedding was only six weeks away, and up until two months ago, they'd been hard-pressed to find something Susan would agree to wear down the aisle.

After seeing Susan in action on several other occasions and watching her parents eventually yield on each issue, Molly suspected the whole gosh-I-just-can't-decide-on-a-dress experience had been a ploy.

Too bad Mr. Sullivan hadn't given in sooner, since the dress had finally arrived and he was going to have to pay through the nose to rush the alterations in time for the wedding.

But as an investment banker, a real-estate mogul and one of Westlake's wealthiest men, he could afford it.

"Let me see the dress," Susan said. "I can't wait to try it on again. Is the alterations lady here yet?"

"Yes," Molly said. "She's in back, just finishing up another pinning."

"But she knows mine has to be done first, right?"

Actually Betty had a first-come-first-served policy. But from what Molly understood, when the order had come through this morning, Susan had told Betty that her father would be willing to pay extra if the job was completed on time.

"I'm sure Mrs. Thistle will have it finished with time to spare," Molly assured her.

Moments later Susan was given the gown, which she quickly carried back to the dressing room. And when she returned, she looked like a fairy-tale princess, even though the bodice was a bit snug and needed to be let out. And the waistline was a little loose and needed taking in.

Still, it was kind of nice seeing Susan in the dress. She and Molly were a size six. And if Molly was going to choose the gown of her dreams, it would be the Vera Wang. Of course, she'd never be able to afford anything that expensive. But ever since it had arrived, she'd been itching to try it on.

She did that sometimes, after closing time, when no one was around to watch. She played dress-up with the bridal gowns, pretended that she'd found her dream mate, that she'd planned her wedding. That her life was complete.

Bertie Thistle, the seamstress who handled most of Betty's alterations, rang up the charges for the last customer with whom she'd been working, then gave Susan her undivided attention.

When Bertie had finished pinning, measuring and making notes, Susan studied her image in the mirror.

"It's absolutely gorgeous," the maid of honor said.

"You're going to be the most talked about bride in the history of Westlake, if not the entire state of New York. And Rick is going to have a hard time keeping his hands off you until the honeymoon."

"What do you think?" Susan asked Molly. "Wasn't this *always* the best choice?"

"It's beautiful," Molly told her. "You'll make a lovely bride."

And she would.

Bertie rang up the charges, and Molly noted that the cost of the alterations, along with the fee to rush the job, was more than a bride on a budget would pay for her gown alone.

But the price didn't seem to faze Susan. She merely signed the receipt without looking it over and paid with her father's credit card. Then she swept across the room to look at herself in the mirror again.

Molly wondered if Susan was more in love with being the bridal belle of Westlake than with the man she was going to marry.

Was she ever going to remove the dress?

Of course, if Molly were a bride-to-be, and the Vera Wang were hers to wear on her own special day, she'd be reluctant to take it off, too.

But ten minutes later the gown had been carefully placed on the special hanger. And Susan had put on her street clothes, a pair of hip-hugging jeans and a form-fitting white T-shirt that looked a size too small but set

off a pair of breasts her father had paid to have en-
hanced—just in time for the wedding.

As Susan and her red-haired friend prepared to leave
the shop, the door swung open and Rico and Colette entered the boutique.

Molly wasn't surprised to see Rico give Susan Sullivan a double take. He was, after all, a bachelor with
an eye for a pretty lady. But she wasn't prepared to see
Susan give him the once-over, too, and struggled with
a weird little green-eyed twinge in her chest.

Moments later the young women left, but the closing glass door didn't silence the giggles and girlish prat-
tle, especially a "Did you see that hottie?" comment.

And why not?

Even dressed casually, Rico could cause a woman's
head to turn, whether she was already spoken for or not.

Today he wore a pair of black jeans and a white knit
shirt that skimmed his wide shoulders and well-defined
pecs, suggesting he was in great physical condition. His
hair, nearly black, had a glossy shine.

Was it any wonder women found the hunk attractive?

And if that woman had once enjoyed the mind-spin-
ning, knee-wobbling pleasure of kissing him…

Molly scolded herself for letting her thoughts drift in
that direction. No matter how moving Rico's kiss had
been, she'd be miserable with a man like him. He was
stubborn, tight-lipped and insisted upon having his own
way—all indications of his refusal to bend. And when

she thought about all the compromises that needed to be made in a happy marriage…

Nope, he was definitely not the man for her.

"We had lunch with Daniel," Colette said. "And while we were out, I decided to bring Rico by the shop and show him the gown I've chosen."

Colette beamed, while Rico looked as though he'd been hog-tied and dragged into the bridal boutique.

"Why don't you try it on for him?" Molly suggested. She knew Rico was going to be a hard sell, but the dress was a perfect fit and wouldn't need any alterations at all.

He might have plenty of qualms about weddings and romance, but he wouldn't be able to deny how lovely his mother looked in that dress.

Colette quickly sorted through the on-hold rack until she found the hanger that held her gown, then headed for the dressing room, leaving Molly alone with Rico.

She glanced at him, saw the way he crossed his arms and shifted his weight to one leg. The poor guy was as uncomfortable in a bridal shop as a sinner who stood front and center in a revival tent, and she couldn't help teasing him. "I hope being in here doesn't cause you to break out in hives. We keep Benadryl on hand just for men like you."

His eyes sparkled like honey in the morning sun. "I am a little itchy." He tossed her a devilish grin. "Do you want to scratch my back?"

She glanced at her nails, filed neatly but longer than she usually kept them. "I might hurt you."

"Promise?"

Sexual awareness sucked the air out of the shop, leaving Molly speechless, her pulse skittering.

Had he meant that as an innuendo? She supposed it didn't matter, because that's exactly the direction her thoughts had gone. Blood pounding, hormones pumping. Hips lifting, back arching, hands clutching. Nails scratching.

She licked her lips, saw him watching her just as intensely as she was watching him, tiptoeing around the chemistry. Flirting with danger.

Okay, so her thoughts had taken a sexual turn. But only because he'd started it.

She crossed her arms. "You aren't making things easy."

"Me?" Rico wasn't going to take all the blame, even though he had let the joke take a sexual turn. But teasing Molly was fun. So was watching her flush, seeing the green of her eyes darken with lust.

"Yes. *You.*"

He couldn't help grinning, nor could he help scanning the length of her.

She wore a simple white cotton blouse and black slacks. Pretty toes with pink polish peered out from a pair of black sandals adorned with silver charms.

His gaze traveled back, past the perfect fit of her pants, the cross of her arms, which had shoved her breasts upward, making them pour from the scooped neckline of her blouse. Back to her pretty face, a flush of color on her cheeks.

He enjoyed razzing her, watching her get riled up. So he tossed her a crooked grin and shrugged one shoulder. "I can't help it. It's the rebel in me."

"I think you're just trying to defuse your discomfort."

"What are you talking about?" he asked. Did she mean the attraction they continued to skate around?

"Well, you definitely feel out of place in a bridal shop." She rested her side against the sales counter in a way he found alluring, but he figured it probably hadn't been intentional.

His gaze returned, albeit slowly, to her eyes.

"Why are you against marriage?" she asked as though unaware of—or unaffected by—his careful assessment. "Or is it just weddings?"

"It's both. And if you take a look at my mom's track record, you ought to understand why."

"That can't be the only reason."

She was probably right. He'd stood by and watched helplessly as his buddy Mac was backhanded by Cupid and dragged through the muck and mire of a painful divorce. And Rico would be damned if he'd put himself in a similar situation. It was too vulnerable of a place to be.

She crossed her arms again, studying him like a shrink who specialized in dealing with the lovelorn. "So when did this aversion to commitment start?"

"Years ago," he admitted. By the time he'd graduated from high school and entered the police academy, he'd completely sworn off marriage.

"That's really sad."

"I don't think so."

"And lonely," she added.

"Hey, that doesn't mean I don't have plenty of women chasing after me—and a few I ran after, too. But anytime one of them got starry-eyed, I backed off."

"I meant lonely in the sense that you don't have anyone special to come home to, anyone to share your problems with, your dreams."

"I don't have any problems," he said. "Or dreams." At least, none that he was willing to share with anyone.

"I don't believe you."

For a moment a wave of loneliness settled over him, but he swept it aside.

There had to be some kind of hex on this place, some romantic mojo that went for the underbelly of a man's heart and weakened him to the point of giving in to rose-colored dreams.

He shrugged. "Some people aren't as needy as others. And they're more realistic."

"And now you're trying to push that hard-hearted philosophy off on your mother."

"Hey, if anyone ought to swear off marriage, it's her. But I'm not completely heartless. I agreed to foot the bill for this thing. But it's not as though she needs a white gown and the whole nine yards."

"It's not white. It's a lovely ivory color. And it looks beautiful with her hair and complexion."

Before Rico could respond, his mother stepped out of the back room, where she'd obviously changed into the dress, and swept into the front of the store.

And Molly had been right.

He'd never see her look prettier. Or happier.

"You look great, Mom." And he meant it.

"Thanks, honey." Her happiness, as fleeting as it might be, lit up the room.

If either one of them expected another comment out of him, they were mistaken. He merely reached into his wallet, whipped out his Visa and handed it to Molly.

"You're going to buy it?" she asked. "No matter what the cost?"

"Cost has never been an issue," he told her.

Hell, Rico had never been able to deny his mom anything. And maybe deep inside that was another thing that scared the ever-lovin' crap out of him. That he'd fall ass over heart in love with a woman and be unable to deny *her* anything either.

When Molly returned his card and handed him the receipt, he'd planned not to even glance at the total, just on principle. But then he worried that she might have tacked on an organist, a five-piece band, a case of champagne and a bushel of rice—or rather birdseed.

But she hadn't.

She'd only rung up the dress, less a thirty percent discount, and added sales tax for a grand total of three hundred and thirteen dollars and forty-seven cents.

It was a lot cheaper than he'd expected.

His buddy Mac's ex-father-in-law hadn't been that lucky. The only-worn-once bridal gown Mac's wife had chosen had cost her old man nearly two grand. And three years later, when the marriage blew to hell, they sold the damn dream dress on eBay for a fraction of the original cost.

"Thank you, Rico." His mom blessed him with a kiss that caused his cheeks to warm.

He shrugged. "It'll be worth it to see you in that dress."

Damn. He felt like a freakin' poet who sat around eating bonbons and writing sonnets all day, which convinced him there truly *was* a hex on this place.

But before anyone could respond, a loud crash and a suspicious crunch sounded from outside.

Oh, crap.

He put away his Visa, shoved his wallet in the rear pocket of his pants, then headed for the door, ready to spit fire.

There was no mistaking the crushing sound of breaking fiberglass.

Someone had hit his car.

Talk about a curse.

What else could go wrong today?

## Chapter Seven

Rico dashed out of the bridal shop and onto the sidewalk, then froze as he spotted the damage to his Corvette.

A wide-eyed teenage girl with long brown hair climbed from an idling blue Chevy Blazer, leaving the driver's door open. She pressed her hand over her mouth as she stared at the bashed-in side of his car.

"I'm *so* sorry. I dropped my lip gloss and was trying to reach it, but… Well, it all happened so fast."

Momentarily struck speechless, all Rico could do was survey the destruction and calculate the time it would take and the cost to repair the body.

"Mister, is this your car?" the teenager asked, crestfallen, her eyes filling with tears.

Rico nodded, swallowing an appropriate expletive. He wished the negligent driver had been a male with his head up his ass rather than a freckle-faced girl with braces, because a blast of temper would feel good about now.

"I have insurance," the teen said, bottom lip quivering.

So did he.

But that wasn't the point. Not just anyone knew how to fix those fiberglass bodies.

Damn. There was no telling what she'd done to the wheel and chassis. He couldn't drive it like that.

Boy, poor old Frank must be rolling over in his satin-lined casket about now.

He'd loved that car, almost as much as he'd loved Rico and his mom. And for some dumb reason, in a goofy, irrational attempt to make a dead man proud, Rico had tracked down Frank's Corvette and had it restored to mint condition.

Yep. Frank ought to be rolling up a storm right now.

"I...uh..." The teenager's brow furrowed, and tears pooled in her eyes. "Gosh, I feel just awful about this."

Rico blew out a ragged sigh, wondering if he could will her not to cry and deciding to give it a try anyway. *Come on. Suck it up, kid.*

A big, sloppy drop ran down her cheek.

Aw, hell. A lot of good his mental telepathy was doing.

She swiped a hand under her eye, catching the watery stream and leaving a black smudge in its place.

They made mascara waterproof. So why was it that some women didn't seem to know that or even care?

The girl looked at the crumpled fiberglass and damaged wheel well, then turned to Rico and grimaced. "My dad's going to kill me. This is the first time he let me take his car into town alone."

"You're just learning how to drive?" Rico asked. If that was the case, this was all her old man's fault. He should have never allowed her out on the public roads.

"No, I'm not like a total beginner. I've had a learner's permit for a couple of months. And I passed my driving test on Friday afternoon."

Always the wise guy when flustered, Rico couldn't help a tongue-in-cheek retort. "Then you've got some experience under your belt, huh?"

Oblivious to his sarcasm, she nodded, then studied his vehicle. "Oh, man. What kind of car is that? I've never seen one of those before."

"It's a '63 Corvette."

"Wow, that's really old. But it looks nice and all clean. You must take really good care of it."

"Yeah, well, it's a vintage model."

"Uh-oh. That means this is going to be really expensive, huh?"

No need to shake up the kid any worse, especially if her old man was going to flip out. "Yeah, well, that's what insurance is for."

Rico's mom, who'd apparently followed him outside, eased forward and spoke to the girl. "Don't worry, honey. The car can be repaired."

Leave it to Colette Garcia to downplay a crisis. Nothing was ever a big deal; there was always an easy fix.

"Would you like to come inside and use the telephone to call your parents?" Molly asked, slipping her arm around the whimpering teen. "Maybe it's best if you let someone drive you home."

"Okay." The girl looked at her Blazer, which was sitting in the middle of the street and idling. "But I can't just leave my car like that."

"I'll move it for you," Rico said.

As his mother led the remorseful teen into the bridal boutique, Molly grabbed his forearm, causing his pulse to go haywire.

Their gazes met, and something he couldn't put his finger on wrapped around them and temporarily drew them together, binding them in some weird way.

Amusement flickered in her eyes. "You surprised the heck out of me, Rico."

"What do you mean?"

"I know how much that car means to you."

Did she? He doubted it. The car was the only connection he still had to Frank. That and the photograph he kept on his desk at the office.

"I expected you to blow up and lose your cool about that accident."

Yeah, well, he almost had. When he'd heard the

crash, he'd been angry. Rip-roaring pissed. After all, he'd been parked, for cripes sake. What kind of idiot couldn't keep their vehicle on the road?

When he'd dashed outside, he'd been ready to lambaste the driver. But he hadn't expected to find a teenage girl who was falling apart at the seams.

He shrugged, which seemed to be his typical response whenever Molly put him on the spot or at a disadvantage.

"It was sweet of you to be sensitive to that poor girl's feelings," she added.

What good would throwing a temper tantrum have done? Her old man was probably going to raise the roof when she got home. Not to mention the cost of her insurance premium was going to skyrocket.

Molly removed her hold on him, then crossed her arms and damn near smirked. "Well, I'll be darned, Rico Garcia. Underneath all that bark and growl, you've got a tender side."

"No, I don't," he snapped.

Before Molly could bring out a brass band on his behalf, he shot her a let's-not-go-there scowl, then strode toward the open door of the Blazer and climbed inside.

As he backed away from his banged-up Corvette, he swore under his breath. Not so much because of the damage to his car but because Molly had accused him of being soft.

And he wasn't.

*She* was soft. So was his mom.

Rico, on the other hand, was just like his father.

Of course, he'd never known the guy, but they had to have been cut from the same bolt of cloth. How else could he explain why he and his mother weren't anything alike? And not just because he was tall and dark, while she was petite and fair. Their very natures were in direct contrast.

Maybe that's why he'd bonded so closely to Frank. To a real man's man. A diesel mechanic, an avid hunter, a one-time offensive linebacker for the New England Patriots until he'd thrown his knee out. A stepfather a boy could look up to, emulate. A guy who had his feet on the ground and kept his head out of the clouds.

Rico shucked the sentimental journey as he parked the teenager's SUV in an empty space in front of the office-supply store, which was two doors down from the bridal boutique.

All the while Molly continued to stand at the curb, watching, waiting. Looking for some imaginary soft spot to surface, he supposed.

Well, she wouldn't find his underbelly.

He wouldn't let her.

Rico had been stuck in bridal hell for over an hour, all the while holding back a torrent of swear words that begged for release.

After the police had arrived to assess the accident, he and the teenager had exchanged names and numbers.

Shortly thereafter, the girl's parents had come to pick her up.

Her father, a gruff-talking guy in his late forties with a beer belly and a two-day-old beard, hadn't been as successful as Rico had been when it came to holding back an initial reaction. Not after he'd taken a look at the vehicle his daughter had crashed into.

He had blurted out a few choice words of his own, until the poor kid had bubbled up in tears and sobs. Then the guy had folded—just as Rico had.

In the meantime, it had taken several calls, including one to Margie at the office, before Rico found a towing service that specialized in vintage cars and had a flatbed truck available.

His mom, of course, might consider this an easy fix. But his car would be out of commission for a while.

When the flatbed arrived and Rico had filled out the customary paperwork and provided a credit card number, he removed his belongings from the Corvette, including a bag of Skittles from the glove box.

"You keep candy in your car?" Molly asked.

"Yeah." He offered the open bag of rainbow-hued fruity chews to her.

"Thanks." She delicately plucked out a single red Skittle.

What was with that? He shook his head in wonderment, then reached in, grabbed a handful for himself and tossed them into his mouth.

He and the bridal consultant didn't even enjoy sweets the same way.

Suddenly curious, he asked, "So what do you keep in *your* glove box?"

"A sewing kit. A nail file. A small first-aid kit."

He handed her the bag again. "What about snacks? You've got to get hungry sometimes."

She plucked out a single yellow Skittle. "Well, I do have some granola bars. But that's in case I don't have time for lunch. Munching isn't a nervous habit for me."

A nervous habit? She made having a sweet tooth sound wimpy, as if it fulfilled some deep-rooted need or something, when the fact was he just liked Skittles. And Reese's Pieces.

He reached back into the bag, snagging another handful. "There's nothing wrong with eating sweets."

"Hey, Mac," the tow-truck driver yelled.

"Yeah?"

"We've got her all loaded up. You want to come and sign off so we can go?"

Sure. Rico popped the candies into his mouth, then strode toward the driver. He scanned the paperwork, then used the pen attached to the clipboard to give his okay.

Moments later, as the truck drove away hauling the battered Corvette to a specialized body shop, Molly returned to the boutique.

Rico followed her, only to find his mom talking to a tall, middle-aged brunette.

"Hello, there," the woman said as she made her way toward him and extended her hand. "You must be Colette's son. I'm Betty Lou Colwell."

Ah. The owner of the shop. And she'd spotted her prey, the guy with the checkbook.

"Rico Garcia." He took her hand in greeting.

He supposed he could have told her it was nice to meet her. But it really wasn't. None of this wedding crap had been his idea. Still, he offered her a polite smile.

Betty practically beamed. "I think it's so sweet of you to agree to pay for your mother's wedding."

Rico forced himself to continue to grin rather than say he was prepared to fight a dog and pony show all the way.

"Can I get you a glass of champagne?" Betty asked him. "We keep it on hand to help our customers celebrate."

"No, thanks." Rico didn't feel like toasting a wedding and engagement he still hadn't fully accepted. And even though the thought of alcohol was tempting and might help take the edge off the lousy day he was having, he didn't think the entire bottle of bubbly would be enough.

"I'll pass on the champagne," he said, reaching for his cell. "But if I can borrow your phone book, I'd appreciate it. I need to call a cab."

"There's no need for that." Betty turned to Molly. "Why don't you drive the Garcias home?"

"I'd be happy to." The blonde tucked a strand of hair behind her ear.

"Oh, no," his mom said. "I'd hate to have you drive us home, Molly. You'd have to come all the way back to work. And since we're going to meet and go over the wedding details later this afternoon, Rico and I can just wait until you get off."

"Well, goodness," Betty interjected. "I had no idea you had an appointment. Why don't you take the rest of the afternoon off, Molly."

"That would be wonderful," his mother said. "See, things always work out for the best."

Rico struggled not to roll his eyes as he clamped his mouth shut.

Molly reached behind the counter for her purse, then led them to the back of the shop and past a room that had a refrigerator, a table and chair, a small TV and a bed.

"Who lives in there?" he asked.

"That's the break room," Molly replied.

"What's the deal? Do you guys get nap breaks?"

She turned around, glanced into the room and laughed. "No, I'm afraid not. About a year ago Betty had gallbladder surgery. But she couldn't stay away from the shop, so she ordered a bed and put it in the lounge. No one uses it, but it's there."

"That's good," Rico said. "I suppose you never know when one of your brides will get faint from bridal excitement and need to lie down."

"I guess we've been lucky," she said with a glimmer

in her eye. "So far, they've all been able to handle their happiness without passing out in the shop."

She turned around and continued out the rear door. Once they stepped outside, she said, "This is where the employees park."

Sure enough, her little Toyota, complete with the artificial rose tied to the antenna with a ribbon, waited near a beat-up green trash bin.

Rico's gaze traveled to the dent in Molly's trunk and the battered rear bumper. She'd told him that she bought the car like that. But after the day he'd been having…

"Mind if I drive?" he asked.

"What's the matter?" Molly asked. "Are you a little jumpy about women drivers today? Or are you still having issues about sitting in the passenger seat?"

Yeah. All of the above.

Especially with a woman like Molly behind the wheel.

Thirty minutes later, after Molly had handed over her keys, Rico drove to Colette's house. And shortly thereafter Daniel arrived in his white late-model Cadillac.

While Molly helped Colette in the kitchen, getting dinner preparations started, Rico kicked back in the living room with Daniel.

Earlier today he'd called an assistant district attorney he knew in Albany and learned that Dr. Daniel Osterhout was indeed a respected forensic dentist. And that the prosecutor's office had been sorry when he'd retired to open a private practice in Westlake.

"You know," Rico said, "I wouldn't give up a career for a woman. Any regrets?"

Daniel shrugged. "I don't know. Some, I guess. I was good at what I did, and in spite of the ugliness of the cases I helped solve, there was some satisfaction, too. Pride in knowing I'd helped get a predator off the streets."

"Why not go back?"

"Because I'm established now." He glanced down at his hands, at his tapered fingers. Then he looked at Rico. "I might call the D.A. and tell him that I'd be willing to do some consulting. But first I'll have to discuss it with your mother."

"My mom has always been very supportive. I'm sure she'd want you to do whatever makes you happy."

"It's important for her to be happy, too. And if she didn't like the idea, I'd just let it drop."

"Even if it meant selling out on what you're good at, on what you've been trained to do?" Rico asked. "That would be too big of a compromise for me."

"A good marriage requires compromise."

"Yeah, I imagine it does. But in some marriages even a compromise doesn't work." Rico thought about Mac, about how hard the poor guy had tried to please his wife, how all his efforts had failed—big-time.

"It sounds as though you've been hurt in the past," Daniel said.

"Nah. Not me." Rico had done his best to avoid putting himself in a position to be slammed. Burned. And besides, he was observant and a fast learner. If someone in front of him fell through an open manhole, he knew enough to walk around it.

Or to cross the street.

As the ladies returned to the living room, the men's conversation ceased. And it was just as well. For his mom's sake, Rico hoped she and Daniel would be happy. But he feared that if Daniel was the only one compromising, there'd be trouble ahead.

"Let's talk about the wedding," his mom said, her face beaming with happiness.

As Molly grabbed her notepad and a pen, Rico spared a glance at Daniel, wondering how he really felt about the big bridal production.

But the man merely grinned and leaned forward, giving the women his undivided attention.

Aw, what the hell. Rico couldn't fight them all.

"We've decided upon Saturday afternoon, June third, at one o'clock in the afternoon at Westlake Community Church." The happy bride-to-be smiled first at her intended, then turned to Rico. "Do you have a problem with that?"

The date? No. But the wedding?

He saw Daniel reach for his mom's hand, watched their fingers interlock. Witnessed the happiness.

The trust.

"No," Rico said. "I don't have a problem with it."

"Good." Molly jotted down something. When she finished, she tossed him a smile.

And before he could lean back in his seat, both women drew him deeper and deeper into the wedding plans.

But when Molly brought up the name of a woman who played the harp for background music, when they'd already settled on a church organist for the ceremony and a trio to play at the reception, Rico couldn't still a grumble.

"What's the matter?" his mom asked.

This was supposed to be a small wedding. Simple. Discreet. At least, that had been *Rico's* plans. And he'd told Molly and his mom as much. So why in the hell were they pushing for the whole shebang?

But he couldn't bring himself to object, to shoot her down when she was damn near ready to burst with excitement.

"Nothing," he said. "The harp will be fine."

"Good. I'm glad we've got it all settled." Molly placed her notepad on the coffee table. "And when I get back to the shop, I'll put a rush on the invitations. That way you can work on them over the weekend and mail them on Monday."

Rico opened his mouth to suggest they slow down a little, to ask Molly not to put a rush on anything. But he figured they'd all—including Daniel—pegged him as Chicken Little, the disillusioned little cluck who thought the sky was falling.

The trouble was, Rico wasn't convinced that the sky wouldn't bust up and rain down on them yet.

But before he knew it, they'd settled all the details.

Then his mom looked at her watch. "I'm afraid dinner won't be ready for another twenty minutes."

Daniel stood and reached out his hand to Rico's mother. "In that case, why don't we take a walk, sweetheart?"

"I'd love to." She turned to Molly. "You don't mind if we step out for a while, do you?"

"Not at all. I was just going to leave."

"I wish you'd stick around for dinner," his mother said. "Chicken in wine sauce is a specialty of mine. And so is the broccoli casserole. And if that's not enough to sway you, I made a deep-dish apple pie for dessert."

Molly laughed. "I'm going to have to invest in a new wardrobe, all a size or two larger, if I don't start passing on your scrumptious desserts."

"I'm not sure how," Rico interjected. "You don't eat more than a bite or two at a time. Sheesh, you even pick at Skittles, and everyone knows they're supposed to be eaten by the handful."

His mom and Daniel chuckled as they strode for the door hand in hand.

Rico watched them go, leaving him and Molly alone in the quiet house. He stole a glance at her, noting that she'd been watching the lovebirds, too.

"It's hard not to be excited for them," Molly said. "I

get this warm, fuzzy glow just seeing them together. They're so much in love."

Rico wasn't so sure about that. But he did know that his mother had never looked happier. He just hoped it would last. Of course, the dentist seemed like a nice guy.

But before he could comment, his cell phone rang.

"Excuse me." He looked at the lighted screen and recognized the number. "Hey, Cowboy. How're are those Californians treating you?"

"All right," the man drawled. "I've been working on that Grimes case for you. And I'm afraid I had a little setback."

Rico's smile faded as he quickly claimed a detached, professional manner. "What's that?"

"David Grimes was in and out of jail over the past twelve years. Last January he went back in on a parole violation. And just a couple of weeks ago he died in a prison fight he'd instigated."

"Damn." Rico glanced at Molly, saw her watching him intently. Did she know he was discussing her case? The death of her father?

Something in the way she studied him said she did.

"And for what it's worth, Grimes's wife was shot and killed during a drug bust about sixteen years ago. A guy who shared a cell with him said she was running packages for a dealer in the neighborhood. Apparently she wasn't really into that scene but got involved just that once to make a little quick cash so she could buy groceries and pay some of the bills."

And she'd paid the ultimate price.

"Grimes hadn't been too happy about being left with the kids, saying they weren't his. But his name was on the birth certificates." Cowboy chuffed. "That guy was a real weasel."

"Boy howdy," Rico said, mimicking one of the Texan's classic remarks.

"But I've got a couple of things to check out," Cowboy said. "And I've also got a hunch."

"Then play it," Rico told him before ending the call and disconnecting the line.

When his eyes lit on Molly's, something passed between them, some sixth sense, some silent communication.

She *knew* he and Cowboy had been talking about her case. And the apprehension in her expression told him that she was expecting to hear some bad news.

"That was Cowboy," he admitted.

"Did he learn anything?"

Yeah. He did. Molly's dad—or the man she thought was her father—was a piece of crap. And if he'd known anything about Lori's whereabouts, the secret had died with him.

So how did Rico break it to her?

And when he did, would she crack? Fall apart?

Rico cleared his throat, then lowered his voice to a soft, gentle, I-hate-to-be-the-one-to-break-it-to-you tone. "Molly, your father died recently. While in prison."

She nodded, as though it hadn't blindsided her, as though she was okay with it.

Was she?

He studied her profile, the way she sat primly on the sofa. Stiff. Her hands poised on her knees as though frozen. Brittle.

But she didn't cry. And for that he was grateful.

Yet he still felt the need to reach out, to touch her. To offer his condolences or something, even if it was a parody on the old *Wizard of Oz* ditty—ding-dong, the bastard's dead.

"So we're back to square one?" She might not have fallen apart, but the emotion was there, thick enough to touch. Heavy enough to unbalance him.

Where was that resilient Pollyanna faith now that he wanted to see it? *Needed* to see it.

He cleared his throat again while he tried to find something to give her hope. "We can always go through the regular channels to find your sister. We've got ways to uncover a closed adoption."

"You know, I never could figure out how they could adopt Lori with only my father's signature. Didn't they have to get my mom's, too? Or was it because she'd been gone for so long that it wasn't necessary?"

Her mom's signature?

Didn't she know?

"Molly, your mother was dead. She couldn't have signed anything."

The color seemed to drain from her face. "She died? When? The last time I saw her, Lori was just a toddler. My mom went out to buy a pack of cigarettes and never came back."

"Is that what your dad told you?" Rico asked.

"No. That's what my mom said when she sent me to bed and grabbed her purse. And when I asked where she was the next morning, my dad told me not to worry about it. That she wasn't coming back."

That's all he said? He just let her think that her mother had deserted her? What a jerk.

Of course, not that her mom would have been a contender for a blue ribbon in motherhood. But her dad should have told Molly the truth. At least the part about her mom being dead.

Now Rico had to be the one to tell her.

"About sixteen years ago your mom got involved in a drug ring—to pay the bills, Cowboy thinks. And during a bust, shots were fired and she was killed."

Her silence was almost overwhelming, yet she managed to hold it together. Although just barely, it seemed.

When she spoke, her voice cracked. "How…hard… do you think it will be to find my sister? And how long do you think it will it take?"

She hadn't mentioned her mom's death, but maybe she couldn't bear to acknowledge it out loud, to expound on her father's betrayal, his lack of honesty. Her mom's misguided attempt to make a fast buck.

"I'm not sure how long it will take, but Cowboy has a hunch, and I told him to play it. Let's see what he has to say next time he calls."

She nodded, then reached out and gripped his forearm, her fingers sending a shiver of heat along his nerve endings and into his bloodstream, jump-starting his pulse.

"I really appreciate your help," she said.

He shrugged. Damn, there it went again. That repetitive, yeah-whatever response he had whenever she struck a sympathetic chord in his chest.

"Don't worry about it," he said. "I'm sure we'll find her."

She glanced down at her lap, brushed an imaginary piece of lint from her slacks. Then she looked at him, snagging him with a soul-stirring gaze. "I *have* to find Lori. If I live to be a hundred, I'll never forget the fear etched on her little face. Or the way she clutched at my sweater, begging me to go, too."

If Rico lived to be a hundred, he'd never forget the depth of emotion on Molly's sweet face, the guilt. The worry. The desperation.

God, where was her faith now? Her rose-colored worldview? Her pain ripped into his chest.

"At one time, we had only each other," she said, her eyes boring into him. "I *need* to know that she's all right, that she's happy, that everything worked out for the good."

"I'm sure she's doing well," Rico said, even though it might not be true.

Molly sniffled, then blew out a weary sigh. "I want her to know that I never stopped loving her, that I never forgot her."

For some crazy reason, Rico had the urge to sweep her into his arms, to offer her a hug, a shoulder to lean on. Yet the whole emotional intensity scared the liver out of him.

The best he could do was to reach for her hand and give it a squeeze.

"Thanks." Her fingers wrapped around his, creating some kind of connection.

He ought to let go, to backpedal. Instead he continued to hold her hand, to stroke his thumb across the soft skin of her wrist.

As the front door opened and his mom and Daniel entered the room, he dropped Molly's hand and stood up.

The connection had unbalanced him, and he was eager to break free.

But he knew one thing. He'd take on the case himself once Cowboy had a solid lead. Maybe that way he could be rid of Molly, rid of the obligation he felt.

And rid of the emotion she stirred.

## Chapter Eight

Molly struggled to make it through dinner without giving way to tears. And not because she felt any actual grief about her father's death.

David Grimes had merely been a sperm donor. He'd never been a daddy. Never tucked her in at night, never listened to bedtime prayers. Never helped her with a math problem—or any other problems, for that matter.

She could actually overlook his neglect, blaming it on the drugs that had screwed up his mind. But there was something he'd done that she would never forgive, something she'd never forget.

He'd turned his back on Lori, on his six-year-old

daughter. Gave her away, as if she'd been a stray dog he'd told someone else to drop off at the pound.

Of course, now Molly had another thing to add to his list of sins, his failures as a father.

He'd never told her that her mother was dead. Instead he'd let the girls think she'd abandoned them, leaving them with a lousy excuse for a parent.

"Would anyone like seconds?" Colette asked, drawing Molly from the dark hole where she'd banished her dismal memories, a place she rarely allowed herself to visit.

"Not me," Daniel said, rubbing his stomach. "I'm saving room for dessert."

"Molly?" Colette asked.

"No, thank you." She tried to smile, but it fell flat.

The state of depression in which she found herself was *so* not like her, and she struggled to climb out of it. To find something to be happy about. But her mind continued to drift to the early years, to the run-down apartment where they'd lived.

She barely remembered her mother, a frail, thin woman who'd smoked an occasional cigarette, savoring each puff she took. A woman who'd sat down at the wobbly dinette table with Molly and Lori, watching as her daughters ate but never fixing herself a bowl or a plate.

Molly had always believed she just wasn't hungry. But she'd been going without so that her children could eat.

Had her mother loved her and Lori all along? Had there been other signs Molly had neglected to see or had forgotten?

Or had she merely blocked the memories after hearing her mother had abandoned them?

"Molly," Colette said, drawing her back to the present, "can you pass the rolls?"

"Sure."

"Am I a lucky man or what?" Daniel asked with a satisfied grin. "My bride-to-be is a wonderful cook."

That was definitely true. Colette could rival Martha Stewart in the kitchen.

"The chicken is delicious," Molly said. At least, that's what she assumed, but for some reason, her taste buds had gone on hiatus and she was just going through the mealtime motions.

"Why, thank you." Colette beamed, obviously thrilled with the compliments that had been bestowed upon her.

Molly stole a glance at Rico. He hadn't waited for his mom to offer seconds. And as he dug into his third helping of the home-cooked meal, he seemed to enjoy every bite.

He'd surprised her today. First with the way he'd handled the poor teenager who'd accidentally run into his Corvette. And then when he'd really thrown her for a loop by reaching for her hand while breaking the news about Cowboy's investigation.

There was more to the man than met the eye. And what met the eye was enough to take her mind off her troubles for a moment or so.

He glanced up, saw her watching him, yet he didn't smile. Instead his gaze reached deep inside of her, asking, *Are you really all right?*

She forced a crooked grin—at least, her lips felt a little uneven. But she hoped it relayed, *Yeah, I'm hanging in there.*

And she was, even though she was struggling to grasp the optimism that had always kept her buoyed in the past. Kept her on top. In control.

When they finished eating and Colette had shooed the men into the living room with the hope that they'd get to know each other better, Molly helped clear the table, then headed for the kitchen.

"You've been exceptionally quiet this evening," Colette said. "Are you all right?"

"I'm fine. I've just got a lot on my mind." *On my heart.* She wished she could tell Colette how she was feeling, but she was confused by it all.

Not by the fact that Lori was as lost as ever. Or by the news that her mother hadn't just disappeared into the night and that her father had failed to tell her she'd gotten involved with his drug underworld, probably just trying to make ends meet.

Molly could certainly understand why those things would push her to the point of tears. But her father's death had also draped a cloak of sadness over her. And *that* she couldn't grasp. The man didn't deserve her grief.

Maybe, after she'd sorted out a few things, after she managed to snag the positive outlook she tried so hard to project, she'd be able to confide in her friend.

"Are you stressed about something?" Colette asked.

Stressed? She was falling apart. But she didn't dare burst the happy bubble Colette was living in right now.

"I'm sorry for daydreaming," Molly told her. "I'm just pondering a few details about your wedding. I want to make sure everything is perfect on your special day."

Colette dried her hands on a dish towel, then gave Molly a gardenia-scented hug. "Thank you."

"You're more than welcome." Molly clung to her friend for a moment longer than necessary, wishing her foster mom lived closer and relishing the maternal role Colette had begun to play in her life. Then she slowly stepped free of the embrace. "I really need to go home."

"But I was planning to put a movie in the DVD player," Colette said. "Don't you think a little romance between Tom Hanks and Meg Ryan would make a nice ending to the day?"

Molly didn't think she could sit through a movie tonight. "I'll have to pass this time. I have some things I need to do this evening. But I'll call you tomorrow, okay?"

"All right."

Molly folded her dish towel and laid it neatly on the

counter, then she headed into the living room to find her purse, her notepad and her day planner.

Rico and Daniel were deep in conversation, but they stopped talking when she entered.

"Are you leaving?" Daniel asked.

"Yes, I'll see you all later. Thanks for dinner, Colette."

As she started for the door, she sensed someone following her and glanced over her shoulder, spotting Rico.

"I'll walk you to the car," he said.

She nodded, words suddenly failing her.

Once outside, he placed a hand on her shoulder, warming her to the bone and setting her senses on edge. "Are you going home to an empty house?"

Her breath caught. "Excuse me?"

Did he want to follow her home? Spend some time alone, just the two of them?

For a moment the blue funk she'd been in seemed to dissipate in the night air, in the silvery moonlight, in the flickering stars.

He raked a hand through his hair. "It's just that I feel like I might have dropped a bomb on you and I… Well, I want to make sure you're okay with it."

A smile came easier this time. "I'm okay. Thanks for asking, though."

They stood like that for a while, awkward with the emotions swirling around them—her melancholy and his sympathy. At least, that's what she told herself it was.

The fact that he was drop-dead gorgeous and she

had this incredible attraction to him was complicating things. So was that unexplored tender side she'd recently spotted in him.

Her arms itched to wrap around his neck, to show him how much she appreciated his attempt to console her and his efforts to find Lori. But she feared an embrace, feared the need it might provoke, the heat. And she was afraid to unleash a slew of complications she wasn't ready for.

Instead she stroked his upper arm, felt the definition of his biceps. "Call me if you hear anything else, all right?"

He nodded.

Her fingers slowly trailed along his arm, as though unwilling to break the tentative bond.

As her hand dropped back to her side, he reached out and cupped her face, his thumb gently stroking her cheek. "We'll find your sister."

"I hope so."

Then he bent and brushed his lips across her brow.

The gentle kiss hadn't been sexual, yet his kindness drew her thoughts in that direction. And something powerful snaked around her heart, too warm to be a threat.

She'd be darned if she knew what it was. Or if she wanted to read anything into it.

Not on a night like this, a night when she wanted to climb into the comfort of her bed and hibernate until her optimism returned and the world righted itself.

She struggled to leave him with an upbeat smile, then opened the car door and slid behind the wheel.

He didn't stop her, but he didn't return to the house either. Not until she'd started the car and driven away.

The tears she'd been holding back slipped down her cheeks, releasing a torrent of grief. Not for her father, she suddenly realized. Or even for the mother she barely remembered. She'd lost them both years ago.

But she grieved a lost childhood and feared that her sister might never be found.

By the time she arrived at the rented house she called home, she'd gone through several tissues she kept in her purse.

She parked in the garage, then grabbed her things and carried them into the house. As she flipped on the light switch, a warm glow settled on her rented home, on the mismatched furniture, the gold-tone carpet that was clean but had seen better days.

Sometimes she wondered if she ought to dig into her savings and purchase a new sofa, a more stylish lamp, a picture for the wall. But her extra money had always been earmarked for finding Lori.

She strode toward the bookshelf, toward the framed photographs of her and the Townsends, and peered at each one.

Her first day of high school.

The Christmas before last, when they'd gotten snowed in at the cabin.

Her foster dad wearing a silly smile and that goofy band-conductor costume for the funky community variety show.

Each photo was a special memory, a display of the good times. The happy days, the people who meant the world to her.

But someone was missing. Someone who should have remained in her life, who should have shared in her happiest moments.

Lori.

Her new parents had taken her away and refused to let her have any contact with Molly.

But Lori was eighteen now, able to decide for herself whether she wanted to have a relationship with the sister who'd tried her best to be both mommy and daddy.

All Molly had to do was find her. Of course, that was easier said than done.

She dumped her things in the easy chair and kicked off her shoes, leaving them on the floor. She was usually neat to a fault, but tonight it didn't matter. She made her way to the bedroom, removed her clothes and put on her favorite flannel pajamas.

Then she climbed into bed and reached underneath the spare pillow, withdrawing the frayed yellow security blanket Lori had always dragged around with her. The blanket she'd left behind. The blanket her new parents hadn't wanted her to have.

Molly held the ratty but precious cloth to her

cheek, closing her eyes and whispering a hope-filled prayer.

Then she willed herself to sleep.

And to wake feeling like herself again.

On Wednesday morning, as Rico prepared to leave his mom's house in a rental car and head back to his office, he cursed his stupidity.

He couldn't believe he'd chased after Molly last night and offered her a shoulder to cry on. He'd actually asked how she was feeling, for cripes sake, when he made a point of not getting emotionally involved with clients. Or with pretty blondes who might expect more out of him than he was willing or able to give.

He had to distance himself from the bridal consultant, from the compulsion to protect her from the reality of her situation. And the best way to do that was to return to the world where he was in total control.

As he zipped his overnight bag shut, his cell phone rang. The number on the display told him it was Cowboy.

Instead of saying hello, he asked, "How's it going?"

"All right," Cowboy said. "I've got a lead in that Grimes case. My hunch was right."

"Oh, yeah? What'd you find out?"

"I took your advice and went back to the old neighborhood last night, checking out that Mexican restaurant, the Laundromat and a newsstand."

"And?"

"A couple of the old-timers remembered Grimes and his daughters. The community kind of looked out for the girls. Felt sorry for them 'cause they were so cute and their old man was such a loser."

That was an understatement.

"Anyway," Cowboy said, "one ol' boy, a fella by the name of Harold, said that an older couple who couldn't have kids adopted Lori. He thought they were either friends or relatives of someone who worked at Rosarita's, the Mexican café."

"You got a name?"

"Miller. Sam or Stan. The old man wasn't sure. But he thinks the woman's name is Carole."

"Are they still in the L.A. area?"

"Nope. They moved out of state. Wisconsin maybe. Or another northern state that gets plenty of snow in the winter. But I'm working on that."

"Good."

"Trouble is," Cowboy said, "that I just got a call from Chuck Clemens. He needs help on a personal matter this time. One he says is critical."

Clemens owned a large biotech firm in southern California and was one of the L.A. office's biggest clients. His company used Garcia and Associates to run their employee background checks.

And Cowboy usually handled the account.

"What's the problem?" Rico asked.

"He's all worked up, claiming that his elderly aunt

is being taken advantage of by the woman who is supposed to be looking after her."

"Go ahead and see to Clemens. Then maybe you can go back to the Grimes case."

"Will do."

The line disconnected.

Rico continued to sit on the bed he'd just made, next to the overnight bag he'd just packed.

Should he share this piece of news with Molly?

Or wait until they had something more solid?

He had the urge to call her, to give her the hope she needed.

But better yet, maybe he ought to drive over to Betty's Bridal on his way out of town.


When Molly awoke in the morning, she felt a little better. The ache in her chest had eased and her tears no longer threatened to spill at any given moment. But she was still far from cheerful.

She made her bed, replacing Lori's blankie under the spare pillow, then headed for the shower, where she shampooed her hair and shaved her legs.

While she finished getting dressed for work—God, it was good to have something to do, someplace to go— she put on her trusty mood music, a CD she'd made of upbeat tunes to pull her out of the dumps.

While having a cup of tea and a bagel, she listened to Gloria Gaynor belt out her blood-pumping, courage-building classic hit, and Molly knew she would survive, too. Feeling better with each song, she glanced at the wall-mounted telephone and thought about calling her foster patents.

She could have called them last night, she supposed. They wouldn't have liked the idea of her spending the night alone when she'd been feeling so low. But they'd been so good to her and worried so much that she never liked to talk to them on those rare occasions when she was feeling mopey.

"Hello," Barbara Townsend said when she picked up the telephone.

"Hi, Mom."

"Molly! It's so good to hear your voice. How are you, honey?"

"I'm fine." And she was—now that it was morning. Now that she'd heard her mom's voice. "How about you two?"

"I just sat down to have a cup of tea, and your father went out to play a round of golf. He sure loves Florida. The weather is lovely. You ought to consider joining us out here."

After Molly turned eighteen, the Townsends had retired and moved from California to New York. Molly had followed them and gotten a job at Betty's. But the winters had played havoc with her foster mom's arthritis, and the couple decided to relocate in Florida, where she'd be more comfortable.

"I wish we lived closer, too," Molly admitted. "But I love my job."

"We know you do, honey. And we're glad about that. When can you come visit again?"

Molly grabbed her day planner and quickly scanned her calendar. "This month isn't going to work. And June is always busy. How about July? I can try to make it on the weekend of the Fourth."

"Great. We'll barbecue."

"I'd like that. And it will give me something to look forward to."

"So tell me," her mother said. "Is there anything new going on? A special man maybe?"

Rico immediately came to mind, yet she struggled to get her thoughts back on track. Back on a viable romantic interest. Like a man who would commit, for one thing. "Not one I'd like to bring home to meet you and Dad. But I'm still looking. And when I find him, you'll be the first to know."

"Well, I've been praying that the right man will come along."

"I know you have, Mom. And I appreciate it." Molly glanced at the kitchen clock. She still had plenty of time before ten, but she didn't think a discussion of what was missing in her life was a good idea. Not today. Not when she was still struggling to stay on top emotionally. "I probably ought to head to work, but I just wanted to hear your voice and make sure you and Dad are doing all right."

"We're fine, honey. Thanks for calling. We love you."

"I love you, too."

When the call ended, Molly locked up the house, then drove to the boutique earlier than usual. Keeping busy never failed to take her mind off her troubles.

She arrived before anyone else and let herself in the back door, then disarmed the alarm and put on a pot of coffee. As she listened to the gurgles and sputters while it brewed, she thought about opening the shop a few minutes early.

What would it hurt?

After unlocking the front door and flipping the Closed sign to Open, she returned to the counter and looked at her appointment book. She'd scheduled to meet Marcia James at eleven o'clock and Vickie Maltby at two.

Minutes before ten the phone rang. She reached for the receiver and answered on the second ring. "Betty's Bridal Boutique."

"Molly?" a panicked voice asked.

"Yes."

"It's Susan Sullivan and I have a major crisis."

"What's the matter?"

"Julie, one of my bridesmaids, just got a full-sleeve tattoo on her arm. It's a scene from *The Lord of the Rings*. Do you have any idea what that looks like?"

"I can imagine."

"But what am I going to do?" the frantic bride-to-be asked. "The dresses are sleeveless, and that great big Frodo on her arm is going to stand out like crazy."

A large shoulder-to-wrist tattoo would probably raise a few brows and stir a few whispers, especially with the conservative people on the Sullivans' guest list.

"This is supposed to be *my* day," Susan lamented. "And everyone is going to be looking at *her*. Why couldn't she have waited until after the wedding?"

It would have been nice if she had, Molly realized. Perhaps Julie had been thoughtless. Or maybe she wanted to steal some attention from the bride. Molly had seen it happen before. Not a brand-new full-on tattoo, of course. But other ploys.

"If Julie were anyone else," Susan said, "I'd tell her and Frodo to take a flying leap off the Two Towers. Then I'd look for someone else who wears a size fourteen. But she's my future sister-in-law, and my fiancé and his parents would probably freak. She's always been their little princess."

"I'm sure it will be all right," Molly said, trying to reassure the young woman who'd grown up as a little princess herself.

"No, it's *not* all right. You'll just have to call the seamstress and have her add sleeves to all the attendants' dresses."

If Molly remembered correctly, the design Susan had chosen didn't have that option. But she didn't dare mention that now. Not until Susan had a chance to cool down a bit. "Let me make a phone call or two."

"If they can't add sleeves, I may have to break Julie's arm so that she has to wear a cast."

Molly knew Susan wasn't serious, just frustrated and prone to dramatics. "Before you feel the need to resort to violence, let me see what I can do."

"Okay, but *please* hurry. This is the worst thing that's ever happened to me. And it's going to *ruin* my wedding. And if I decide to give her a piece of my mind, it'll probably cause a divorce before we've actually said our vows."

Molly hung up the phone, then sorted through the file, looking for the Sullivan work order. But before she could find it, the door swung open.

She glanced up as a dark-haired hunk swaggered into the room, the morning sun casting a glow at his back, producing a princely aura.

Rico.

A combination of embarrassment and excitement warmed her cheeks. Had he come to see her?

"I was just heading back to the city with a loaner car from the insurance company," he said. "But I got another call from Cowboy and I thought I'd stop by and give you a bit of news that might make you feel a little better."

She walked out from behind the counter, brushing her hands against her hips. "Thanks. I could use some good news. What did you find out?"

"We have a lead on the couple who adopted your sister."

Molly was speechless.

*Finally.* After all these years. She had a connection to Lori.

"Who are they?" she asked, moving closer to Rico. "Where can I find them?"

"We think their name is Miller and that they're friends or relatives of someone who worked at Rosarita's. Cowboy is going to check into it."

Molly's heart soared with hope, with appreciation, with feelings she couldn't express.

Without a thought, she gave him a spontaneous hug. "You have no idea how much I appreciate all your help."

The unexpected embrace sent Rico's heart rate hammering, his desire racing. And in spite of a knee-jerk reaction to take off at a dead run, he slipped his arms around her, felt her breasts pressed against his chest.

Instead of stepping back, as he certainly should, he savored the sweet scent of her body lotion. Something that reminded him of peaches and cream.

In spite of his better judgment, he held her close and felt the silky strands of her hair against his chin.

As he stroked her back, his fingers slid along the slinky material of her green blouse, a garment that caressed her gentle curves, and he fought the urge to explore the rest of her.

She slowly loosened her hold. "Thank you *so* much."

For what? he wondered, his brain taking a momentary detour and allowing his libido to kick up its heels.

Senses swirling, testosterone soaring, blood pumping, he fought for control of his body, his lust, and slowly dropped his arms.

"No problem," he said, referring to his efforts to find her sister. But there was a hell of a problem with the mounting urge to kiss her, to taste her, to…

Their gazes locked, and he found it a little hard to breathe, hard to speak.

She nibbled on her bottom lip, as though suddenly aware that her blast of appreciation had taken a sexual turn.

At least, it had for him.

He had to get out of here. Out of the bridal shop. Out of Molly's reach.

Switching to business mode—or at least giving it the old college try—he reached into his jacket pocket and withdrew his card. "I don't expect to be back until the wedding. So call me if you need anything…you know, for a check. A credit card. Whatever."

"All right."

Then he turned and walked away, managing not to break into that dead run he'd pondered earlier.

As the door closed behind him, he sucked in a breath of freedom, glad he'd escaped.

But a whisper of peaches followed him all the way to Manhattan.

## *Chapter Nine*

On Saturday afternoon, the third of June, Molly stood at the back of Westlake Community Church.

Just minutes before, she'd checked on Colette and her matron of honor, Jane Grider, Daniel's widowed sister and only living relative. The women had been nearly dressed and ready to walk down the aisle.

So now Molly made one last scan of the church, mentally checking off each item on her list.

She'd lain awake for hours last night going over all the details. And by hook or by crook she would make sure everything was perfect.

But not just for her friend Colette, a woman who deserved a special wedding to kick off a future filled with love and happiness. Molly strove to make this particular wedding perfect for herself, too. As a means of bolstering the faith she'd placed in her own dream. That someday *her* prince would come.

The flowers—blue and lavender hydrangeas—adorned the altar, where a young acolyte carefully lit each white tapered candle until the flames flickered. Along the pews, ribbons and bows hung in alignment. And as if God was making His own presence and pleasure known, the afternoon sun sparkled through a single stained-glass window on the east wall, casting a rainbow-colored blessing upon the gathering.

The organist, a plump, matronly woman wearing a lavender dress with a floral print, played a medley of songs as the last of the guests trickled in. Most people had already arrived and filled the first eight rows on both sides of the small, quaint church that had been built in the 1800s and boasted the original altar and pulpit.

If Molly closed her eyes, she could almost feel the love that had been shared here over the years, hear the voices singing hymns of praise.

But Molly didn't have time to daydream. Or to tarry.

She checked her watch. Ten minutes until one. Realizing she ought to check on the groom, she slipped along the side of the church and made her way to the choir room, where Daniel and Rico had been sent to get ready. She rapped lightly on the door.

"Come in," Rico said.

Molly entered, only to find him alone, struggling with his tie. A shank of dark hair had fallen onto his forehead, and he wore a boyish frown.

She couldn't help staring, admiring him. And she realized something utterly amazing.

In that state of nervous frustration and imperfection, Rico Garcia was even more gorgeous, more appealing than he'd ever been before.

"Where's Daniel?" she asked.

"In the bathroom. *Again.* The poor guy's a nervous wreck. And not because he's got cold feet, which I could understand. But he's a real goner." Rico shook his head. "Can you believe this guy? He's testified in court under tough cross-examinations and held his own. But he's a mess today. He's afraid he'll stutter or stammer, that he'll screw up the words he wrote to say, that he'll lose it and get all sentimental."

Molly thought that was sweet.

Rico fussed with the skewed tie a bit more, then threw up his hands. "Dammit. I hate these monkey suits."

*Daniel* was nervous?

A grin tugged at her lips as she made her way toward him. "Here, let me."

For once he seemed willing to yield, to take the passenger seat and let Molly take over. And if she thought it wouldn't have set him in a bad mood, she would have teased him about it.

Instead she lifted her hands and fiddled with his collar as his musky, mountain-fresh scent made her mind spin, her pulse race.

She'd helped many men adjust their ties or cummerbunds in the past, but this time her own fingers stiffened and rebelled. She tried to keep her reaction to herself, since she didn't need to add any more emotional turmoil to the rush of sexual awareness heating up the small room.

Somehow she managed to straighten his tie, yet her attention was drawn back to the lock of hair that lay on his forehead. She brushed it back in place with her fingers.

"There you go," she said, her voice soft yet husky.

Their eyes met, and silence filled the room, releasing a flurry of pheromones and hormones, urges and desire.

She hadn't seen Rico in three weeks, although they'd talked on the telephone once—about bills and deposits he needed to pay. But they'd never discussed the stimulating embrace they'd shared in the bridal boutique. Or the attraction that a three-week separation hadn't dulled, one that seemed to have grown dangerously strong. An attraction that was right this moment nearly overwhelming.

Before either of them could speak or respond, the door creaked open and Daniel walked into the room.

Thank goodness. The cavalry had arrived. And just in the nick of time.

She turned and smiled at the dapper groom. "You look great, Doctor."

"Thanks." He flashed a sheepish grin. "Does my nervousness show?"

"Not a bit." She offered him a gentle smile, one meant to soothe his nerves. "Are you guys ready?"

Daniel reached into the inside pocket of his jacket and withdrew a folded piece of paper, scanning the words he'd written from his heart. Then he glanced up and nodded.

"Then I'll check on the bride. And if she's ready, we'll get the ceremony under way."

Five minutes later Dr. Osterhout strode out the side door and stood at his post near the altar. His arms hung loosely at his sides, his fingers fidgeting along the strip of satin on his slacks, as he gazed toward the double doors where Colette would make her entrance.

Rico stood beside Daniel, hands clasped in front of him and projecting total control. Yet he appeared stiff to Molly. Uncomfortable in his tux, as well as the church, she suspected.

But at least the cynical P.I. was being a good sport. She had to give him credit for that.

The organist began to play the introductory chords of the wedding march, and all heads turned, looking back, awaiting the entrance of the bride.

Jane, Daniel's sister and a beautiful woman with hair that was more salt than pepper, wore a blue chiffon gown in a classic style. As she stepped down the aisle, she nodded graciously to her right and her left, obviously far more at ease than the men. Her happiness for the bride and groom was apparent in every graceful stride, in her joy-filled smile.

The musical chords altered, indicating it was time for the bride to meet her future husband, to say their vows. To promise to love each other until the end of time.

Tears welled in Molly's eyes as she stood at the back of the church rather than the seat Colette had reserved for her. She preferred to man her position, overseeing the wedding like a professional. At the reception she would let down her hair—figuratively speaking. She'd worked too hard to sweep up her hair in a neat, professional twist.

As Collette started down the aisle, she never looked lovelier, and not just because her hair had been coiffed to perfection. It was the joy on her face, the love in her eyes and the hope in her heart that made all the difference. And as far as Molly was concerned, there'd never been a prettier bride.

Colette glanced in her direction and mouthed a thank you.

"My pleasure," Molly whispered back.

Then Colette continued on her way to the man she would pledge to love for the rest of her life.

When the couple stood before the minister, the ceremony began, and fifteen minutes later Colette and Daniel Osterhout were pronounced man and wife.

The tears that had brimmed in Molly's eyes slipped

down her cheeks as she watched the beaming newly-weds walk gaily down the aisle and out the front door, ready to meet their family and friends. The photographer's flash had a magical effect as he caught another glimpse of the special day on film.

As Rico escorted Jane down the aisle, he caught Molly's gaze and watched as she wiped her eyes with a handkerchief she'd brought for the occasion.

*Happy now?* he seemed to ask, his ever-present cynicism busting to break free.

She lifted her chin, crossed her arms and shot him a grin. Yes, she was proud of herself, proud of the way the wedding had turned out.

But she wouldn't exactly say she was happy. Not until she'd found her sister.

In less than an hour Rico planned to peel off his damn tuxedo and head back to the city. He'd done his part by wearing it in the first place, by standing at Daniel's side, by meeting each of his mother's friends—both old and new.

He'd smiled through an obscene number of photographs, signed the license as a witness and paid the minister. Then he'd climbed into a black limousine with his mom, new stepfather and...well, technically Jane was his aunt. Not that he needed or wanted one at this stage in his life.

The luxurious Lincoln had led a caravan of cars to

the Westlake Country Club, where the reception was held in the St. Augustine Room. There Rico had munched on the fancy hors d'oeuvres and drank his share of scotch from the hosted bar.

He'd watched as his mom and Daniel had cut into a three-tiered cake and fed themselves little bites. What a goofy custom that was.

There wasn't much more for him to do other than offer a toast. Molly had wanted him to do it earlier, but he thought it would make a nice send-off. A hint that the party was over and people ought to go home, leaving him free to finally get out of this damned monkey suit.

As several waitresses carried trays of champagne flutes and offered them to the guests, Rico snagged one for himself. And while the leader of the three-piece band asked for everyone's attention, Rico made his way to the microphone.

He thanked everyone for attending, then made the toast short and sweet. "If there were ever two people who deserve to live happily ever after, it's Dr. Daniel Osterhout and his beautiful bride, Colette."

As everyone cheered and clinked their glasses, Molly flashed him a genuine smile. *Not bad,* it seemed to say. *Not bad at all.*

Knowing he'd pleased her sent a surprising swell of warmth through his chest and slapped a smile on his face. And he couldn't help striding toward her.

She was especially pretty today, with her hair swept

up in a prim but flattering style and wearing a classy teal gown that set off the green flecks in her eyes.

"Did I behave?" he asked.

She nodded, eyes glistening. "You pulled it off, in spite of your skepticism about love and forever."

He shrugged. "I hope they find it."

"I'm sure they will."

Rico fought the urge to roll his eyes, to revert back to the skepticism that kept him afloat. Balanced. In control.

It's not that he didn't want to see his mom happy, that he wasn't hopeful that things would work out for her this time. But there were no guarantees in life. None whatsoever. And he didn't see the point in getting all mushy and unrealistic.

But for some reason he kept his mouth shut, refusing to upset Molly today. He wasn't sure why, though. Maybe because he liked seeing her looking pleased, happy.

Damn, she had a beautiful smile.

Before he could excuse himself and break free of a rare sentimental streak, his cell phone vibrated in his pocket. A part of him wanted to ignore it, but Mac was working in the Chicago office this week. And he'd been having a problem with the fine line he had to toe on his current case. He had to be careful not to break the law during his investigation of a philandering husband who also happened to be a judge.

He glanced at the display. Nope. Not Mac. This call was from Cowboy.

"Will you excuse me?" he asked Molly.

She nodded, and he stepped outside, onto the patio that overlooked the ninth green.

"What's up?" he asked his friend and associate.

"We hit another wall."

In Molly's case, Rico realized, since just last week Cowboy had wrapped up his work for Chuck Clemens, uncovering enough about the elderly woman's care-taker to provoke a criminal investigation by local law enforcement.

He listened intently, asking a couple of questions and not getting the answers he wanted.

As the line disconnected, he realized he would have to break the news to Molly.

And that regardless of his wish to keep her smiling today, he was about to tilt her rose-colored world on its axis.

Molly stood just inside the main entrance of the country club, looking out at the wedding guests who'd gathered where the idling limousine was parked curb-side, the passenger door open.

The limo would take Colette and Daniel to Manhat-tan, where they would spend their wedding night at the Waldorf-Astoria.

Then, tomorrow morning, the newlyweds would fly out of JFK, headed for Munich and a three-week honeymoon that also would take them to Austria and Switzerland.

Rico hadn't returned from taking his phone call, and Molly wondered whether she should go out to the patio and tell him his mother was going to be leaving soon.

But before she could make a move, Colette, who'd changed out of her gown and into a cream-colored suit, hurried toward her.

"Thank you for everything," the happy bride said, wrapping Molly in a warm embrace. "You were right, everything was picture-book perfect."

"Just like the rest of your life is going to be," Molly added.

"Hey," Rico said as he strode toward them. "Looks like you're off."

Colette released Molly and slipped her arms around her son. "Thank you for making this possible. You don't know how much it means to me. Or rather, to us."

"You're welcome," he said. "Now be safe. And have fun in Europe."

When Daniel made his way to his bride, he extended his arm to Rico and shook hands. "I'll take good care of your mother."

"I'll hold you to it," Rico said.

Then the happy couple headed out the door and into a rain of birdseed.

Molly and Rico stood together, inside looking out, and watched as Daniel and Colette climbed into the limo.

As they drove away, Rico placed a hand on Molly's

shoulder, sending a ripple of heat through her bloodstream and kicking her heart rate up a notch.

"Come on," he said, turning her around and leading her through the country club. "You're off duty. Let me buy you a drink."

For some reason it seemed like the most natural thing in the world to do.

"All right," she said. "Thanks."

As Rico led Molly into the lounge and up to the bar, he asked what she'd like to drink, then ordered a scotch and water for himself and a white wine for her.

He wanted privacy for this conversation, too, so he carried the glasses out to the empty patio, where he'd spoken to Cowboy, and held a chair for her.

She offered him a smile, then took a seat.

He placed their drinks on the glass-topped table, then sat in the chair next to her, wondering where to start and deciding on a slow and easy approach.

"It was a lovely wedding," she said, her voice a bit reflective. "Don't you think?"

"Yeah. I guess it was okay, as far as weddings go." He took a sip of his drink, wishing his usual ease at conversing with women would kick in. But this wasn't anything like casually hitting on an attractive lady he'd just met.

She fingered the spindle of her wineglass yet didn't lift it to her lips.

"I…uh…" He took a breath and started over. "That call I received a while back was from Cowboy."

Her eyes widened. "Has he found Lori?"

"Not yet." He cleared his throat, trying to figure out the best way to tell her, then deciding to start at the beginning. "Apparently Sam and Carole Miller had seen you and Lori go into Rosarita's a couple of times. And their hearts went out to you both, but especially to Lori, since she was so young."

A pensive expression stole across Molly's face. "Before we were separated, Lori had been a sweet six-year-old with long white-blond hair and a missing front tooth."

Molly had been eleven, Rico realized. And probably at that gawky pre-adolescent stage that wasn't as appealing to the Millers.

His chest tightened as he thought about the disappointment she must have felt. The sadness. The rejection.

But what a lovely young woman she'd grown into.

"Lori's an adult now," Molly said. "A college student probably, with big plans for her future."

He struggled to find the right words, to tell her that a higher education probably wasn't in the cards for her younger sister. Not at this point.

"Every single day since she's been gone," Molly continued, "I've hoped and prayed that she was placed with a loving family like the Townsends. And that her parents provided her with all the things I was blessed with, all the things other children sometimes take for granted."

"From what Cowboy has gathered, the Millers were decent people," Rico admitted. "And when they heard your father had gone to prison and you kids were placed with protective services, they contacted him and asked him to let them have Lori. Permanently."

"They thought I'd be too difficult to handle," she said, her voice soft, revealing the pain she still carried, the disappointment her optimism hid.

The Millers had been wrong, he suspected. Molly probably never gave her foster parents a bit of trouble.

"You know," she said, "I'll never forget the day they took Lori away. It was gray and overcast."

He figured it had been branded in her memory.

"We'd had pancakes for breakfast." She offered him a wry smile. "Weird that I would remember that, too."

Not really. He still remembered exactly what he was doing when he heard that his stepfather had been shot. That Frank wasn't coming home. Rico had been eating a grilled cheese sandwich and watching the Discovery Channel. A documentary on the lioness and her hunting skills.

The irony of that still amazed him, especially since he suspected a female had shot his stepdad in a case of mistaken identity. But no one had been able to pin it on her.

So Molly was right. Memories could be weird.

"The social worker had to pry Lori away," Molly said. "Then she placed her in one of those white government-issue sedans and drove away, leaving me more alone, more afraid, more brokenhearted than I'd ever been before."

Or since, he suspected.

"How long did you live in the receiving home?" he asked, hoping that it hadn't been years and at the same time regretting that his curiosity might stir up her tears.

"A couple of months after Lori left, Don and Barbara Townsend—an older, childless couple who loved kids— decided to become foster parents. And it was my lucky day." She offered him a warm smile, one that suggested the weepies were over. "From then on, I got three square meals a day and a bedroom of my own. But better than that, I finally had someone who loved me."

He was glad—for her sake.

Molly was the kind of woman who needed to love and be loved. Just like his mother.

"I was so happy to be with the Townsends, to finally have a home with heat in the winter and food in the pantry, that I went out of my way to be obedient, to do whatever they asked me to do."

"Lori went to a good home, too," he said. "But Carole died a couple of years later. And when Sam remarried, it was to a much younger woman."

A woman who was barely in her twenties and too young to parent a teenage stepdaughter.

"And?" Molly asked, as though sensing that he was holding back.

"The details are still a bit sketchy, but your sister ran

away about six or seven months ago. And they haven't seen her since."

"She was still a minor then." Molly's eyes filled with tears, and her bottom lip quivered, as though she was aware of the danger to a naive young woman on the streets.

Her fear and disappointment were palpable, and it damn near turned Rico inside out. He reached for her hand, finding it cold, limp.

"Ah, Molly." He stood, then pulled her to her feet, taking her in his arms. "Don't worry. Cowboy is good at uncovering things. He's got a sixth sense about this kind of stuff. We'll find her."

She looked up at him, tears welling in those grief-stricken eyes. "Are you sure?"

"Yeah. I'm sure." God, now she even had him trying to paint a rosy picture, a happy-ever-after ending.

She clung to him, and he stroked her back, comforting her in a way his mother used to do when he was young and hurting.

Then he cupped her cheeks and lifted her gaze to his. "Do you hear me? We'll find her."

She nodded, that buoyant faith shoving the worry from her expression.

For a moment their gazes locked.

And when she flashed him a wobbly smile, he bent to place a kiss across her brow in a friendly fashion. The way he'd done before. But for some crazy reason, this time a swirl of emotion that had very little to do with compassion—or friendship—swept over him.

He brushed his lips against hers instead, once, twice.

This was crazy. Foolish. Dangerous.

But at this very moment all he wanted to do was to hold Molly in his arms, to roam his hands along the contour of her back, to pull her hips flush against a growing erection. To kiss her thoroughly, deeply. To taste her, to explore her mouth with his tongue.

And he'd deal with the consequences later.

## Chapter Ten

Rico's surprise kiss nearly knocked Molly to her knees, but she didn't push him away.

She couldn't. His scent was too mesmerizing, his embrace too intoxicating.

Instead she closed her eyes and held on tight, caught in a rush of desire.

Her lips parted and the kiss intensified. Their tongues mated, tasting and seeking, savoring the thrill of exploration while sparking a hunger deep inside.

As Rico ran his hands along the slope of her back, along her hips, branding her with his touch, she leaned into him. He moaned, then gripped her bottom with both hands and pulled her against him.

She whimpered, losing herself in his arms, in his kiss. She laced her fingers through his hair, through the silky curls she longed to touch.

Reason suggested she pull away, yield to her better judgment, but she was lost in the most arousing kiss she'd ever experienced, one even more heated than the one they'd shared outside Antonio's.

Their first kiss had been his attempt to tease her, to taunt her. But this one was filled with compassion, as well as heat. And the combination of emotion and desire nearly turned her heart on end.

Had she misjudged this man? Did he have a tender heart that he'd been hiding?

Could he be the one she'd been waiting for?

Rico pulled his mouth from hers, his breathing ragged and hot. He momentarily rested his head against hers, then slowly dropped his arms, releasing her. Ending the mind-numbing, soul-stirring kiss.

"I…uh…" He raked a hand through his hair, mussing the strands more than her fingers had. "I'm sorry about that. I guess you could say I'm not very good at offering consolation."

Had he only been consoling her? Surely there had to have been more going on that that. Hadn't there?

She was too stunned to respond. And with the way her heart was racing, she didn't trust herself to speak.

"I didn't mean anything by it," he added.

He could have fooled her. She could have sworn that

he was offering her the world with that kiss, laying his kingdom at her feet. And his claim that it meant nothing sent a flood of disappointment rippling through her.

But she wasn't going to get weepy or defensive.

His attempt at consolation may have left her weak and turned her brains to mush and her knees to rubber, but she wouldn't let him know. Not if it killed her—which it might, if she ever kissed him like that again.

So she conjured an unaffected smile. "Well, you know how chemistry is. You never can trust it to leave well enough alone."

The lie warmed her cheeks and left an ache in her chest.

There'd been more than hormones at work, at least on her part. There'd been some emotional involvement, too, not to mention a crazy burst of hope that she might have found a prince among men.

But how stupid was that?

"Yeah," he said. "Chemistry can be a real bitch." Then he cleared his throat. "Anyway, I was trying to make you feel better and got carried away."

That was an understatement.

She glanced through the glass patio doors, saw the country club staff cleaning up after the reception.

Had anyone witnessed their heated embrace? Witnessed the bridal consultant making out with the son of the bride?

That was one for the rumor mill.

"What I should have said," Rico admitted, "was that

your sister's disappearance may seem like a big set-back, but we'll find her."

*We'll* find her.

It was nice to think of Rico as being on her side, as part of a team, even if that's as far as things went between them. And if she could slow her raging pulse and rein in a few misguided romantic fantasies, she'd be content with that.

"We're not going to throw in the towel yet," he added. "Cowboy plans to interview her friends. Maybe someone knows where she might be. Or where she was headed."

Molly nodded, her senses reeling. But if Cowboy was going to look for her sister, she wanted to go along, too. Should she ask to take time off from work?

The timing couldn't be worse, though. Susan Sullivan's upcoming wedding would be one of the most elaborate ceremonies and receptions the community had seen in years. And it was only three weeks away.

Could she ask Betty to handle things from here on out?

After all, rather than trying to coerce the seamstress into working nonstop to create sleeves on six gowns before the wedding or suggesting Susan and the other five ladies get matching tattoos, Molly had come up with the idea of matching wraps.

She hadn't seen the finished product yet, nor had she any idea how Susan would feel about the new look of her bridesmaids.

"If it makes you feel better," Rico said, "I'll have Cowboy remain in Minnesota until he gets a lead on your sister's whereabouts."

That *did* make her feel better. But it also made her more determined to be an active part of the search. "Maybe I ought to go and help Cowboy look for her."

A knot formed in Rico's gut. He didn't like that idea one bit. Cowboy was a real ladies' man and would charm the panties off a woman like Molly.

And Rico couldn't let Molly get within arm's distance of Trenton James "Cowboy" Whittaker, good buddy and trusted associate or not.

And how hypocritical was that?

For a guy who had decided to protect Molly, even from himself, he'd lost his head and kissed her again. And talk about arousing. Damn. He'd been tempted to drag her off to the shelter of the weeping willows on the tenth green and let his libido run rampant.

"I don't think it's a good idea if you go to Minnesota," he responded. "You'd probably just hinder Cowboy's investigation." Although, *distract* him was more accurate.

She smiled, apparently taking hold of her optimistic streak. "Lori and I were very close, and I'd like to think we have one of those psychic bonds that sisters have. Maybe my instincts will be helpful."

"I don't believe in that psychic stuff." He did, however, put a lot of faith in instincts—his, anyway. Cow-

boy's, too. And his gut said to sever all ties to Molly before he did something he would regret.

Of course, he also had a sense of honor. And he'd
promised to find Lori.

Molly fingered the side of her head, feeling a loose
strand their heated embrace had dislodged and tucking
it behind her ear. "Well, whether you believe it or not,
there's something special between Lori and I, so I'll call
Betty this evening and tell her I need to go out of town
for a few days." She inhaled a deep breath, then slowly
blew it out. "Of course, first I have to make sure I've
figured out a way to effectively hide a tattoo."

Molly had a tattoo?

Wow. She seemed too conservative for something like
that. But she was also proving to be a little unpredictable.

So where was the tattoo? Obviously not in plain sight.

Could it be on a back hip? Or maybe on a thigh?

He couldn't quell his rising curiosity or suppress a
grin. "Where are you hiding it? I'd like to see it."

She crossed her arms and frowned like a substitute
schoolteacher who'd been blindsided by a mischievous
little boy. "Are you kidding? *I* don't have a tattoo. One
of the bridal attendants in an upcoming wedding just got
a big one that goes from her shoulder to her wrist. And
the bride flipped out and wants to cover it up."

"How about one of those little wraps or capes you
women wear?"

"That's what I suggested and I have the seamstress

working on them now. I just hope the bride will approve of the final product."

"Sounds like she has two choices," Rico said. "She can be content with a bunch of caped bridesmaids or paint on a happy face and make the best of it."

Her eyes brightened. "You're right. Sometimes I take too much of this stuff to heart. Thanks for putting it in perspective. You're entirely right."

He wasn't sure why she was thanking him. It seemed like a no-brainer to him.

She smiled, and her arms fidgeted at her side as though she wanted to give him another big hug and a kiss in appreciation—something that ought to make him run for the eighteenth hole and beyond.

But just the thought that she might be willing to go another round was more appealing than it should be.

The sexual arousal he felt for Molly hadn't abated in the least and was actually growing stronger with each damn kiss they shared.

He really ought to let her go to Minnesota and help Cowboy on the case—even if it meant she'd be swept off her feet within the first twenty-four hours of meeting the handsome, slow-talking Texan.

"I'll tell you what," Rico said, coming up with a better idea and a way to compromise. "I'll fly to Minneapolis and join Cowboy in the search. Together we'll make quick work of finding Lori."

"Good," she said, eyes bright. "I'll go, too."

"That's not necessary."

"Oh, but it is. I've been waiting twelve years to see my sister again. And I want to be there when you find her."

Rico started to object, to tell her to stay out of the way and leave the detective work to professionals. But when he looked in her eyes and saw years of grief reflected in her hopeful gaze, he didn't have the guts to say no.

He'd have to call the office. And the airlines.

Silently he cursed his weakness.

"When do we leave?" she asked.

He paused for a moment, hoping she'd change her mind, that he'd sprout a pair of huevos when it came to dealing with the pretty blond bridal consultant. But in the meantime, his mouth overstepped his better judgment.

"We'll fly out first thing on Monday morning."

At 8:37 a.m. on Monday, Molly met Rico at the Continental Airlines ticket counter, where they checked in their bags and received boarding passes. Rico's nonstop scowl let her know he wasn't happy about something.

Maybe he wasn't a morning person. Or perhaps someone had set him off earlier.

The fact that her presence might be bothering him crossed her mind, but she chose not to embrace an idea like that. He'd get over it. Eventually.

Two hours and very few words later, they boarded the plane that would take them to Minneapolis. Molly pulled out the airline magazine from the seat pocket in front of her and made an attempt to complete the cross-word puzzle.

About the time the plane began its descent into Minneapolis, Rico elbowed her and nodded at the package of nuts she hadn't opened. "Are you going to eat those?"

She handed them to him, hoping a little protein would improve his mood.

"Thanks." He tore into the pack and emptied them into his hand. "I thought they were going to serve us breakfast on this flight and not just beverage service."

He should have eaten before he'd come—*she* had.

By the time the captain turned on the seat-belt sign and the flight attendants began to make their final rounds, Rico finally started to come around. "Cowboy is picking us up."

"I'm looking forward to meeting him."

Rico made a little gruntlike noise, and her resolve to keep quiet and let his mood run its course crumbled.

"Are you angry at me?" she asked.

"No. Why?"

"Because you're in a bad mood, and it's beginning to affect mine. So I was going to suggest you tell me what's bothering you so we can get past it."

"Sorry. I'm just used to traveling alone. That's all. I do better when I'm by myself."

She had a feeling that's the same way he preferred

to travel through life—alone. And that's why he wasn't happy about bringing her along.

Well, too bad.

After they touched down in Minneapolis and collected their luggage off the baggage carousel, Rico led her outside to wait for his associate.

"There he is." Rico pointed to a white Cadillac Escalade that pulled to the curb.

A tall man wearing a black cowboy hat, faded jeans, a white button-down shirt and a brown suede jacket got out of the driver's seat and opened up the back. As the men shook hands, Molly couldn't help studying Rico's good-looking associate.

The fair-haired man didn't look anything like Rico, who boasted a strong resemblance to his Latino roots. But they both, at least initially, projected a princely aura. Of course, Rico's almost militant bachelor philosophy had quickly extinguished his.

Still, both men made a dream-provoking first impression on a woman. And Molly found their obvious friendship interesting, especially with their different mannerisms. Rico was so East Coast. And Cowboy's demeanor shouted Texas from the top of his felt hat to the soles of his fancy boots.

After his greeting with Rico, Cowboy turned to Molly, broke into a grin and swept his hat from his head, revealing mussed hair that had an appeal in and of itself.

"Howdy, ma'am," he said in an intriguing Southern drawl. "You look a lot like your sister."

Molly's carry-on bag slipped from her grip and landed on the sidewalk. "You've already met Lori?"

"No, ma'am. Not in person. But I saw a couple of pictures at her folks' house. And she's a pretty gal, the spittin' image of you."

Rico stooped to pick up her bag. Meaning to set his associate straight, he said, "Cowboy, let me introduce you to Molly Townsend, the woman we're *working* for."

The Texan tossed her a grin. "Trenton James Whittaker at your service. I answer to TJ at home and Cowboy when I'm not."

Then he picked up her bigger bag and stacked it in the back, next to Rico's. "You ready to go, boss?"

"Yeah." Rico hadn't been too keen on introducing Cowboy and Molly and he'd be damned if he knew why the idea grated on him as much as it did.

Maybe because he knew how badly she needed to be protected. After all, Cowboy was as much of a confirmed bachelor as Rico. And Molly had been hurt enough in the past. She didn't need her heart broken or even bruised by either one of them. And Cowboy hadn't figured that out yet.

Not that the man wasn't honorable. He'd respect the client-investigator relationship. And he was always up front about his no-commitments philosophy when it came to dating.

Cowboy might have a way of enticing women of all ages, but there was so much more to the man than charm and good looks.

Texas born and bred, Trenton James Whittaker had walked into Garcia and Associates about five years ago, offering his services. His résumé had been hard to beat, and after a background check, Rico had hired him and put him to work.

It was Rico who'd first dubbed him Cowboy, and the nickname stuck since the man stood out like a sore thumb in Manhattan.

His speech and mannerisms often gave the impression that he was a backwoods detective, but that couldn't be any further from the truth. Cowboy was sharp and intuitive. And he was a damn good P.I. who loved his job and the thrill of the chase.

When the car had been loaded, Rico opened the door for Molly, allowing her to sit in the backseat, then he climbed in front, across from Cowboy.

As they pulled away from the curb, Cowboy rested his left wrist on the steering wheel and shot Rico a glance. "Just this morning I got the name and address of another one of Lori's friends. Her name is Rebecca Mason and she lives in Faribault. I thought that if you don't mind going to work before we check you into the hotel, we could give the little gal a visit."

"That sounds good to me," Molly said from her seat in back.

Rico turned around and their gazes met. Her eyes seemed to seek his acquiescence. But hell, that's what they were here for—to find Molly's sister. "Let's go to Faribault."

Twenty minutes later they pulled in front of a white wood-frame house on a quiet, tree-lined street.

"Sam Miller quizzed Rebecca a couple of times in the past," Cowboy said as he turned off the ignition. "But she'd repeatedly told Miller that she didn't know anything. But from what I've gathered, the two of them were thick as thieves."

"Maybe she'll open up to us," Rico said. "Or give us another clue."

Three doors swung open as they climbed out the vehicle, then shut in unison as they headed to the front door, with Molly taking up the rear.

Rico knocked, and a round-faced brunette in her late teens answered.

"Excuse me, ma'am." Cowboy shot her his trademark smile. "We're looking for Miz Rebecca Mason."

The young woman stood near the doorjamb and held tightly to the edge of the door, as though ready to slam it in their faces. "That's me. I'm Becky Mason."

"I heard you're a friend of Lori Miller," Cowboy said.

"Yeah. I used to be. But she doesn't live around here anymore."

Molly stepped forward, out of the shadow of the men. "Hi, Becky. I'm Lori's sister, Molly. We were separated as children, and I've missed her *so* much. I've never stopped hoping to find her again. And so I've hired a couple of private investigators to help me trace her."

"Oh, my God." Becky opened the door, allowing them inside. "I can't believe it. And you even look a lot like her."

"I know she ran away from home," Molly said, stepping into the small, cozy living room and taking the lead in the investigation, as Rico and Cowboy followed behind. "But do you know where she went?"

"Her dad and stepmom were giving her a lot of grief, so she ran away. I told her she could stay here, but she was afraid her dad would try to force her to go back home and she hated it there. Her stepmom was a real witch." Becky flipped a strand of long brown hair over her shoulder. "My folks would kill me if they knew, but we have a cabin near the Wisconsin border. It's vacant after Christmas, so I gave her directions and the key."

"Is that where I can find her?" Molly asked.

Becky shook her head. "No, she left there nearly two weeks ago."

"Do you know where she went?" Molly asked.

"She was going to call me and let me have an address or phone number once she got a job and found a place to live. I haven't heard from her yet, but from what she told me, she was going to California."

The news seemed to take Molly aback. "Why?"

"She was going to look for you."

* * *

Ten minutes later Rico left his business card with Becky, telling her to call him the minute she heard anything from Lori. Then he followed Molly and Cowboy to the SUV and climbed inside.

"See?" Molly tapped Rico on the shoulder. When he turned in his seat, she smiled. "It's good that I came along. Becky would have kept Lori's secret, like she has for the last six months, but she trusted me. Maybe because she saw the family resemblance."

Yeah. That part was true. But he didn't want to tell Molly that he didn't like the idea of her sister being on the streets of L.A. with only two hundred and forty dollars cash on her, which is the amount Becky had given her before dropping her off at the Greyhound station.

There were predators that hung out at bus depots, especially in big cities like Los Angeles, just waiting for naive young women who'd run away from home. But he wasn't going to mention that to Molly, who seemed to think she was on the verge of a happy-ever-after ending with her sister.

He hoped it all worked out. For her sake. Lori's, too. But he was too much of a realist to disregard the darker possibilities. And in the past week or two Lori had probably gone through most of her money and would be getting desperate soon.

Once in the SUV, he whipped out his cell phone and

called Margie, asking her to book a flight to Los Angeles for him and Molly. Then he covered the mouthpiece and spoke to Cowboy. "Molly and I can take the case from here."

"You sure?" Cowboy asked.

"Yeah. You did all the footwork. It should be a piece of cake now, especially if Becky is right and Lori gives her a call in the next couple of days like she's supposed to."

"All right," Cowboy said, his hands resting easily on the steering wheel, his eyes on the road. "Then I'll probably head back to Texas for a couple of days. My uncle Pete is having a birthday party next weekend, and even the family black sheep ought to make a showing."

In no time at all they arrived at the Marriott, where Margie had made reservations for Rico and Molly. The location was perfect since it was just minutes from the airport and offered a shuttle service.

As Rico climbed out of the luxury SUV, he met Cowboy at the back to unload the luggage. "Thanks again for all your help."

"No problem." As Cowboy lifted Molly's bulky suitcase from the vehicle, she joined them, and he tossed her a hey-good-lookin' grin.

"I sure appreciate your help," Molly told him. "I'll have to figure out a way to make it up to you someday."

"Well, now," the Texan said with a chuckle. "I always

like it when a pretty lady owes me something. But you can buy me a bourbon the next time we meet. That'll take care of it."

"Then I'll buy you two for good measure."

Cowboy shook Rico's hand, then tipped his Stetson to Molly and flashed her another charming, footloose grin. "It was a pleasure, ma'am."

"Thank you. It was nice meeting you, too."

Then Cowboy got back into his vehicle and drove away.

Rico and Molly started for the hotel lobby. Out of the corner of his eye he saw her glance over her shoulder and take one last look at the departing Texan. And it chapped Rico's hide, for some dumb reason. After all, Cowboy would be back in Texas about the time Rico and Molly got to California.

But he couldn't keep a lid on it. "Cowboy's not your type, Mollyanna."

She stiffened, although he wasn't sure if it was because of the nickname or her reaction to being caught staring after the departing Texan.

"What are you talking about?" she asked.

"He's a handsome hunk. But he doesn't commit to one woman either."

"Do you think I'm getting the hots for your business associate?"

He didn't know what he thought, other than the fact that it bothered the hell out of him just to have those two eyeballing each other and tossing flirtatious smiles back and forth. "I was just giving you a heads-up. Cowboy has broken his share of hearts in the past. Not on purpose, but some women think he's easy pickings. And he's not looking to settle down."

"I wasn't flirting."

Well, maybe not blatantly.

As they checked in, the registration clerk—an older man in his late fifties—handed them two keys. "We've got you in three-twenty-six and three-twenty-eight. The rooms are adjoining, like you requested."

Rico hadn't requested the rooms to be adjoining. Margie must have, which seemed a bit odd. She should know he wouldn't try to put the moves on a client. Okay, so he had already overstepped his personal boundaries. But from now on he was determined to keep his hands—and his lips—to himself.

There was a way to make the rooms separate and secure, too—if he wanted to.

Thoughts of bedtime crept over him, making him wonder about nightly rituals, about the kind of clothing she slept in, the material.

Flannel? Brushed cotton maybe? Those little boxer shorts and tank tops? Or would a romantic woman like her choose satin or silk?

Hell. The woman was so enigmatic that she might even sleep in the raw, like he did.

"Come on," she said. "The elevators are over here."

"Wait a minute. I need to stop by the gift shop."

"Did you forget to pack something?" Miss Gotta-Have-My-Day-Planner asked.

"Nope. I'm starving and I want a candy bar."

She followed him inside the little store, then perused the souvenirs and magazines while he loaded up on a supply of Snickers, Reese's Peanut Butter Cups and a couple of Starbursts.

When he'd paid the tab, he wandered over to the rack that held various drugstore sundry items. As she studied the shelf of hand lotions and sampled a Polynesian scent in a tester, he looked overhead and spotted the condoms.

Not that he'd been looking for them. But once they came to mind, his thoughts returned to nighttime, to room service and candlelight, to open doors and turned-down beds. To a silk-clad—or better yet, bare-skinned—beauty.

Oh, for cripes sake. He grumbled under his breath and tried remind himself of the words he'd spoken to Cowboy, of the unspoken rules of a professional.

*Let me introduce you to Molly Townsend, the woman we're working for.*

"What do you think?" Molly asked as she lifted her wrist for him to smell.

He caught a heady whiff of plumeria blossoms, a scent that stirred his senses and his imagination more than he cared to admit.

"It's okay," he lied. Then he scanned the shelf, spotting a green-and-white bottle with a big gardenia on the front and snatching it for her. "How about this one?"

She took a look at the label and opened the lid. "It smells an awful lot like the fragrance your mother wears."

Yeah. He knew that. It's why he'd suggested it in the first place.

Hell, if they were going to spend an indefinite amount of time in close proximity, he'd rather have her smell like his mother, a scent that would be a real turn-off, romantically speaking.

Because he damn sure didn't want her wearing something that would remind him of ocean breezes, flickering tiki lights and making love on a patch of grass along a deserted stretch of beach.

## Chapter Eleven

That evening Molly knocked lightly on the door that separated her room from Rico's.

When he answered, with his hair mussed, his chest bare and the top button of his black slacks undone, her breath caught.

"What's up?" he asked.

She'd gotten bored watching television and had decided to order a pay-per-view movie. Then, on a whim, she'd decided to ask Rico if he'd like to join her.

But seeing him look so casual, as though he'd kicked off his shoes and had been sprawled on the bed…

She shrugged, mimicking his unaffected response to some of her questions in the past. "I'm…uh…going to rent a movie and thought you might want to watch it with me."

His lips quirked and his eyes glimmered. "You're not going to try and coerce mc into a chick flick, are you? I'm big on kick-ass action. You know, shoot-'em-ups, blood and guts."

"I don't suppose we could compromise? Maybe watch a feature-length cartoon?"

He laughed. "Maybe we can find something we can both decide on. What the heck. Your room or mine?"

A strange urge to see where he was going to sleep swept over her, a curiosity about where he'd kicked back and made himself at home. A desire to see the real Rico Garcia, relaxed and with his defenses down.

"It really doesn't matter, but to be honest, I'm tired of looking at my four walls. Why don't we watch the movie in your room?"

He swung open the door, letting her in to a place where he'd obviously marked his masculine territory.

A single king-size bed, with its pale blue-and-beige-plaid comforter crumpled from the weight of his body, took up the bulk of the room. Or maybe that was merely her focal point.

He'd uncovered the pillows and piled them on top of each other against the headboard, making a comfy seat for watching TV. Or had he been reading?

Nope. There was no sign of a book or magazine.

Candy wrappers littered the nightstand, next to a half-full glass of water.

He grabbed the TV clicker, then surfed until he found the preview channel. There were a couple of movies Molly would have liked to have seen, which Rico promptly nixed.

They settled on an action flick starring Brad Pitt because Molly suspected, with Nicole Kidman as a costar, there would be romance involved. A little something for both of them, she decided.

More than an hour into the movie, in which Molly had become surprisingly engrossed, Rico got up and stretched. Then he went over to the desk and picked up the room-service menu. "I'm going to call and order some dinner brought up. I'm starving. Do you want something, too?"

She was beginning to think the man was always hungry. "Sure. Let me see what they have."

Rico ordered the steak sandwich, medium rare, with fries. And Molly requested a cup of chicken noodle soup and a dinner salad, with ranch dressing on the side.

"Red or white?" he asked.

"Excuse me?"

"Wine."

"Oh. Either, I suppose." It didn't matter. Since she was in a strange city and not going to be sleeping in her own bed, she hoped a little wine might help her unwind.

Rather than asking for two glasses, Rico ordered a bottle of Merlot.

She couldn't help wondering if he had trouble sleeping away from home, too.

Once he hung up the phone, they went back to the movie, most of which was set in a Colombian jungle, where Nicole played a missionary who had devoted herself to a group of orphans. Her character added a gentle light to an otherwise dark and violent story.

The love scene, however, was just as sultry, just as steamy as the tropical setting.

As the actors escaped to the back side of a waterfall, they succumbed to openmouthed kisses, while their hands slid along slick flesh, groping, exploring. The roar of the pounding water couldn't mask the heavy breathing, a gasp, a moan, a whimper.

The passion displayed on the screen permeated the confines of Rico's hotel room, heating the air, sparking the ever-present pheromones in a wild frenzy.

As they sat at opposite ends of the king-size bed, Molly struggled not to risk a peek at Rico.

All right. So she stole a couple of surreptitious glances at the man, who was even more appealing half-dressed and a bit rumpled.

In the not-so-distant past her dream mate had borne a resemblance to Brad Pitt, decked out in black-tie, Academy Awards-ceremony splendor.

But when had that image begun to pale?

Probably the moment Rico had swept into her life in a vintage Corvette.

She glanced at the TV, caught a flash of a hip, a thigh. Hands seeking, caressing.

Boy, oh boy, it was getting warm in here.

Unable to help herself, she shot another glance at Rico. Was that love scene having any kind of effect on him?

If Molly could have excused herself without appearing as though she was getting all hot and bothered by the lovers on the screen, she would have. But if truth be told, she wanted to stay. The memory of the kisses she and Rico had shared was doing a real number on her. And she wondered whether he would kiss her again. If he even wanted to.

She could imagine it taking place in the shower, with the spray thundering down on them like a jungle waterfall.

Oh, for Pete's sake. She crossed her legs, then tucked a strand of hair behind her ear. Then she checked a cuticle on her right index finger.

By the time the movie credits were rolling along and she'd fidgeted enough to count as a day's worth of aerobic exercise, the bellman knocked and Rico opened the door.

The man wheeled in a table with their dinner, a bottle of red wine and a single red rose in a bud vase. "Where do you want me to put this, sir?"

Rico nodded toward the balcony, then stood and whipped out his wallet. "It's awfully warm and stuffy in here."

Was it too presumptuous of her to guess that the walls had closed in on him, too? That she wasn't the only one who'd gotten a little hot and flustered?

The bellman set up dinner for two on the patio, placing the bud base in the center of the table, then opening the bottle of wine. As he prepared to wheel the cart back to the hotel restaurant, Rico signed the tab, then slipped the guy an additional tip.

"Thank you, sir." The man cast a warm smile, then gave a slight bow as he stepped out of the room.

"Come on," Rico said, "let's eat."

Molly joined him on the patio, under the spell of a full moon and a scatter of stars that sparkled like fairy dust.

Great. Just what she needed. More atmosphere.

Yet Rico seemed oblivious to it all.

They ate in silence, yet she was nearly overwhelmed with sexual awareness, with the presence of the ruggedly handsome man sitting across from her, his tousled hair, his light whisper of a beard.

And of the rumpled bed just steps away.

She placed her napkin in her lap, then spooned a little dressing over her salad.

"It's a pretty night," he said, gazing at the sky.

She nodded. "Yes, it is. The stars are especially bright."

Rico poured her a glass of wine, then filled one for himself. He lifted it in a toast but didn't comment.

Neither did she.

How could she, when she didn't know what she should be celebrating or wishing for?

A relationship with Rico would be fiery but brief. And where would that leave her?

They both took a drink. As his eyes met hers, something settled over them, something that suggested he was just as aware of her as she was of him.

But she wouldn't go there.

She couldn't. Not if she planned to find her sister without the unnecessary emotional entanglements a short-lived, star-crossed affair with a man like Rico might create.

So in an attempt to defuse some of the sexual tension, to get her thoughts on solid ground, she asked, "Are you feeling better about your mom and Daniel?"

The question seemed to take him aback. "You mean about them getting married?"

"Yes. And about them being truly happy and in love."

"I don't know. I guess their feelings seem legit."

"You saw Daniel struggle with his nerves on Saturday. And you witnessed his excitement."

Rico shrugged.

"Have you ever seen your mom happier?" she asked.

"Not lately. But she's a lot easier to read than a lot of people. She wears her emotions on her sleeve." He slid Molly a crooked grin. "Like you do, Mollyanna."

Her feelings?

Or the desire that continued to plague her?

She decided to let that part of his comment drop and pounce on the nickname he'd given her. "I'm not sure that I like you calling me Mollyanna."

"Why?"

"I think having an optimistic outlook in life is an asset, in which case I'd be pleased with the name. But you see optimism as a flaw. So when you call me that, there's a negative connotation."

He took another sip of wine. "It's a way of pointing out our differences, actually. And I really don't mean it as an insult."

"I hope I never become jaded like you."

"Me, too. That would mean you'd have to learn the hard way."

"Learn what?"

He reached for a steak fry, leaned back in his seat and popped it into his mouth. She wasn't sure if he was savoring his meal or contemplating a response.

"That there's no such thing as fairy-tale endings," he finally said. "I've seen too many unfaithful spouses in my business, not to mention having experienced a parade of stepfathers in my life. People think they're in love right up to and during the wedding ceremony, but time changes things—like feelings. Like love and commitments."

"I've seen couples who have a special relationship, born of love, respect, honor." Her foster parents, the Townsends, for one.

"Yeah, but even in those rare instances, fate intervenes. Either way, all marriages, like all love affairs, come to an end."

"Eventually, yes. But don't you think people should reach for happiness and cherish the time they do have together?"

He shrugged, something he did a lot when she asked him questions.

Did he respond like that when she got too close to the things that made him tick?

"You adored Frank," she said, bringing up his first stepfather, the man Colette and Rico had both loved. The man who'd been tragically shot in a hunting accident. "Do you think your life would have been better if you'd never known him, never had those few years with him?"

Rico didn't shrug. In fact, he didn't answer for so long that she wondered if he'd heard her. Or if he was ignoring her for some reason.

"I…" He cleared his throat, then his voice got a bit louder. "I'm not sure. Frank was the only father I knew and I damn near worshipped the ground he walked on. So did my mom. But to have him die like that, when I wasn't ready to let him go…"

The rest of his words, along with the small crack in his armor that allowed her a glimpse into his heart, disappeared like a wisp of smoke into the night air. But not before giving Molly a rare insight, a vision of a grieving little boy who'd desperately wanted a father to round out his family.

And he'd been disappointed time and again.

No wonder he was afraid of marriage and commitment. Rico was afraid to risk his heart.

"Frank's death was certainly a tragedy," she said, "but he didn't leave you and your mother on purpose."

"No," Rico said. "He was murdered."

For a moment Molly didn't know how to respond. "I thought—or at least, your mother told me—that it was a freak accident. A stray bullet from some other hunter's gun."

"That's what she chooses to believe. But Frank and his friend Joe Rainville were hunting on private property, and no one else was supposed to be out there but them."

"You think his buddy shot him?"

"No. The bullets didn't match. And besides, Joe was pretty torn up by Frank's death." Rico took another drink, a slow, steady sip. "But at the time Joe had just ended an extramarital affair."

She wasn't sure what that had to do with it.

"Joe was cheating on his wife," Rico said, tossing her a humorless grin as though pointing out another broken vow, another failed marriage, one more commitment that had bitten the dust.

"People choose to cheat and they choose not to. It's a matter of honor." She poked her fork at a cherry tomato, dipped it in the ranch dressing and popped it into her mouth. "The trick is finding a spouse who is honorable."

"Actually," Rico said, "the reason I brought that

up was because Joe was later stalked and killed by his wacky lover in a *Fatal Attraction*-style murder." He leaned back in his chair, then caught her gaze. "I think the woman intended to shoot Joe that day and missed."

"Have the police investigated that possibility?" she asked.

"Yes, and they came up empty-handed. After I became a cop, I tried to get them to open up the cold case. And then I did some investigating on my own. But all I got was a strong gut feeling that won't hold up in court."

Rico had a lot of reasons to be jaded, she supposed, reasons to be cynical when it came to love. And in spite of his negativity, her heart went out to him.

For a moment she pondered what she was feeling for him.

Understanding. Sympathy. And definitely attraction.

But was she starting to fall for him? For a man who was a self-proclaimed bachelor with no intention of settling down?

It saddened her to think of Rico remaining alone all his life. Of course, a special woman might come along someday, a woman who would make him believe in love.

In spite of herself, Molly wondered whether she was that woman.

But in her dreams, her prince didn't have baggage.

Shouldn't that matter?

"You know," she said, standing, "I'm really getting tired and I'd better turn in for the night."

"All right. I'm going to sit out here and finish this bottle of wine."

Grieving for Frank? she wondered. For the love he'd lost and had never been able to replace?

She reached out and ran a hand along his cheek, felt the roughness of his beard. The bristle that could easily be shaved away if he chose to run a razor over it.

He grabbed her hand, held it so fast that, even if she'd wanted to, she couldn't pull it away. Her skin tingled. Her pulse throbbed. Her heart raced.

For a moment time stalled and they were caught up in something more powerful than either of them. It seemed as if they were at a crossroads, as though Rico was ready to make a choice, a change.

Ready to take a chance.

With her?

She couldn't stifle the hope that he was ready to risk it all.

God help her, she was.

"Sometimes you have to step beyond the past," she told him, "so you can embrace the future."

His gaze caught hers for a moment, as though her words had struck their mark.

Then he slowly released her hand, letting her go. Rejecting the love she was prepared to offer him. "You need to clean those rose-colored glasses, Mollyanna."

She could have taken offense, marched off in a huff of anger and frustration. Surrendered her optimism. But instead she bent and placed a kiss upon his brow.

Then she turned and slowly walked away.


Rico watched Molly pass through the sliding door into his room, then disappear into hers and close the door.

He fingered the spot above his brow where she'd kissed him.

And what had he done?

Just sat there like a man mired in quicksand.

For some dumb reason, he thought about following her, sensing he could say or do something that would bring her back and allow them to start over.

But is that what he really wanted?

Where would their passion lead?

Nowhere but trouble.

Hell, that movie they'd watched, the one with a libido-stirring love scene, had him all worked up, but not because he'd been drooling over Nicole Kidman. It had been Molly he'd wanted.

And she'd wanted him, too.

She'd been practically squirming in her seat, sneaking glances at him rather than the TV.

That in itself had been reason to let her go, to remind himself that he didn't get involved with clients, especially with a woman who had a romantic streak a mile long and needed a man who would commit.

He grabbed the neck of the bottle and refilled his glass. Then he took a steady sip and glanced at the moon, a cold, gray, desolate piece of rock that looked down at him.

Had he done them both a favor? Or had he made a big mistake?

It was going to be a hell of a long night, just knowing Molly was lying in bed alone.

And knowing she was merely a knock away.

At noon the next day Rico and Molly landed in Los Angeles and followed a throng of people to baggage claim.

Neither one of them mentioned the conversation they'd shared last night or the movie they'd seen, so it made no sense to broach the sexual tension that had lingered even after Molly had gone to bed and left Rico to wallow in it alone.

For hours he'd rued his decision to let her go, even though he'd been looking out for her—*and his*—best interests.

God knew, a brief love affair wouldn't do either of them any good.

But his libido wasn't buying it.

If he didn't find her sister soon, he might not be able to make the right choice next time.

Or had it been the wrong choice? He still wasn't entirely sure.

When they stopped by the rental-car desk to pick up

the vehicle Margie had ordered for him, Rico was given the keys to a late-model white Corvette.

At home he drove his vintage model for sentimental reasons more than anything. And on the road he preferred an SUV.

Margie knew that.

Occasionally he might want a flashy car. But that was only if he was going undercover and pretending to be someone he wasn't, someone who preferred a sports car or wanted to be noticed.

But not on this trip, when he'd be driving around the Los Angeles suburb of Lakeridge, in the barrio known as El Nopal.

Rico would have objected about the Corvette but figured it had something to do with the availability of the GPS he asked Margie to request on his rented vehicles.

"I see you like fast cars," Molly said.

Her false assumption didn't sit well, so the rebel in him responded. "Fast cars, fast women. You sure have me pegged."

He figured it was safer that way, letting her think he was shallow. So he took the keys and headed for the parking stall, where the sleek white 'Vette waited.

When they'd loaded the car and he'd revved the engine, Molly asked, "Where are we going from here?"

"To the hotel. And then I thought we'd head out to El Nopal and check out your old neighborhood. Maybe Lori went there in search of you."

"I'm not sure if she would remember the name of the city where we lived, let alone find it," Molly said. "She was only six when she moved away. And I have very few memories of that time in my life."

The time before her mother had died.

She'd told him to let go of the past, but maybe she ought to face more of hers. He nearly commented but held his tongue on that issue.

Instead he said, "Don't forget that Lori's adoptive parents knew someone from this area. She's apt to be aware of Lakeridge, El Nopal and Rosarita's. And besides, she's had nearly a two-week jump on us."

An hour and ten minutes later they'd checked into the Starlight Palms, a four-star hotel in the better area of the city, and were headed to Oleander Boulevard, the street where Molly used to live.

"The apartment building is on the right," Molly said, "next to the parking structure. They've fixed it up some."

It must have really been a rat trap twelve years ago, Rico decided, since it didn't look too good to him now.

The oatmeal-colored stucco had taken on a steady dusting of highway exhaust and grime. The brown trim was chipped, and bars secured the windows.

A couple of blocks down, just past the Laundromat, Molly pointed out a lone brick building with a white sign in front. Red and green cursive lettering spelled out Rosarita's.

"There it is," she said, referring to the restaurant

with ties to the Millers. "There's parking in front and in the back."

As Rico slowed the vehicle and turned on his right-hand blinker, she added, "It looks the same."

Shabby and in need of paint, like the rest of the neighborhood, he decided. But the saving grace was the small blue-and-white poster in the front window boasting an A rating by the health department.

That was comforting, especially since Rico was hungry and wanted a couple of tacos.

Besides, he figured the employees would be more talkative if they thought he and Molly were customers.

After a beer delivery truck lumbered by, making it safe for him to turn right, Rico pulled into the entrance and drove around the building. On the west side, about halfway down, he pulled into the second row, next to a dented blue Dumpster. But before he could shut off the ignition and unbuckle his seat belt, Molly was out of the car and headed to the front of the restaurant, undoubtedly eager to get inside and find her sister.

He caught up with her near the cash register, where she waited for someone to return to duty.

When a young twenty-something woman with a round-faced smile arrived, Rico took the lead. "Two for lunch."

"Of course. Please come this way." She escorted them to a table by the window, handed them two menus, then smiled proudly, as if it were the best seat in the house.

If Rico stretched his neck, he could see the front of his car and the Dumpster. So much for having a view.

Moments later a busboy who didn't seem to be able to understand English gave them water, chips, salsa and marinated carrot slices.

Rico, always hungry, dug right in.

The waiter, an older man who stood about five-three, whipped out a small notepad and asked if they'd decided on an order. Rico requested the cheese-enchiladas-and-beef-taco combination. And Molly asked for a chicken tostada a la carte.

Before the waiter could return to the kitchen with their order, Molly said, "Excuse me, sir. Is Mrs. Ramirez still the owner?"

"No, she passed on a couple of years ago."

"Have you worked here very long?" she asked.

"About five years."

Rico wanted to remind her that this was *his* investigation and she was only along for the ride, but he kept his mouth shut.

"I'm looking for someone who has worked here for twelve years or more," she said.

The waiter nodded. "Maria has been here for a very long time. I'll go get her."

A couple of minutes later an older, heavyset woman waddled over to their table. "I'm Maria. Paco said you want to talk to me."

Molly introduced herself and asked if she remembered the apartment fire and the two little girls who used to stop by and get menudo on Sunday afternoons and burritos on weeknights.

"I remember the fire," Maria said.

"One of the girls was a pretty little blonde," Molly added. "She was adopted by the Miller family."

"Oh, *si*," the woman said. "I remember now. *Que lastima.* It was so sad. Those poor children were dressed in rags, yet the older girl took very good care of the little one. They were adopted by the Millers, a nice couple who used to eat here every Thursday night."

"No," Molly said, "only the youngest was adopted. I'm the older girl. And I'd really like to find my sister Lori. I heard she might be looking for me."

"I have not seen her," the woman said. "And I'm here all the time. I'm pretty sure she has not been around."

Rico pulled out his business card, and Molly reached for her purse. She fumbled at the back of her chair, obviously feeling for a strap that wasn't there and coming up empty-handed.

"Oh, shoot. I was in such a hurry, I left my purse in the car."

"I have a pen," Maria said, pulling one out of her pocket.

Molly took Rico's card, turned it around and wrote a quick note to Lori. Then handed it back to the older woman. "If she comes in, please give that to her and have her call us."

"I'll do that." Maria slid it into the pocket. "Now if you'll excuse me, I need to go back to work."

As the woman walked away, Molly scooted back her chair. "I'd better go out to the car and get my things."

"It's locked," Rico said. "So your purse is probably safe."

"I'm more concerned about my day planner than my cash or credit cards," Molly said. "I can't live without it."

He shot her a grin. "Typical control freak."

"Maybe so, but no one can say I'm not organized or efficient."

"I'll bet you make lists, too."

"You say that like it's a problem."

"Not for me." Rico reached into his pocket for the keys. "I'll go get your stuff. Why don't you wait here for our food?"

"Don't bother." She stood. "I'll get it."

He was going to object, but he had a pretty good view of the parking lot.

So he handed her the keys.

"Thanks. I'll be right back." As Molly made her way out of the café, a wave of disappointment settled over her, but she did her best to shrug it off. Surely Lori would find this place. And when she was given Rico's card, they'd be able to eventually connect.

Her shoes crunched along the dirty roadway, but a noise drew her attention. And so did a small shadow from near the back of the Corvette.

"Excuse me," she said.

A hooded form glanced up.

"Hey!" she yelled, hoping to startle him and let him know there was a witness. "Get away from that car."

The form froze, yet she could see the eyes, wide and wary. Uneasy, as though not wanting to get caught.

She couldn't very well stand by and watch someone deface the rental car, so she proceeded ahead, not intending to be a hero but hoping to scare off whoever it was.

Of course, it was also possible the person was sick or injured.

The figure, apparently male and wearing a black hooded sweatshirt, jumped up and took off at a dead run. But before Molly could get two steps closer to survey the back end of the car for damage, someone grabbed her by the arm.

"Are you crazy?" Rico asked, spinning her around. His voice sounded angry, yet worry filled his eyes. "What do you think you're doing?"

"That guy was hanging out behind the car. He might have planned to steal it."

"So what? The damn car can be replaced, and you…"

*Can't.*

He hadn't finished his sentence, but Molly sensed the words that hung in the silence. The unspoken emotion.

But before she could even contemplate a response, a little whimper sounded from behind the car, drawing her attention.

What in the world was that?

"Wait a minute," Rico said. "You stay here. I'll go take a look."

Molly knew she ought to appreciate his valiant attempt to protect her, but she recognized the sound—the despair, the need—and was drawn to it.

She pulled away from Rico's grasp and followed the sad little cry to the back of the Corvette.

## Chapter Twelve

Rico followed Molly to the back of the 'Vette, where she stooped and reached for a small, whimpering ball of filthy, matted fur.

"Oh, you poor thing." She struggled to release a small dog from the old electrical cord that had been wrapped around its neck and tied to the bumper. "Hold still, sweetie. I've got you."

When she managed to free the critter, she held it against what had been a pretty white blouse—one that would soon be wrinkled and dirty.

Then she glanced at Rico with hopeful eyes. "Do you think that maybe that guy couldn't afford to keep his dog any longer and hoped we'd take care of it?"

On the contrary. Rico thought the psycho lurking behind the car had hoped the driver would take off down the road and drag the poor mutt to its death. But he hated to dump an ugly scenario like that on Mollyanna. So he decided to shield her in the same way Daniel had protected Rico's mom from the realities of his forensic cases.

"No, that jerk *definitely* did not want that dog." Rico scanned the parking lot, noting the guy had disappeared.

People who abused animals often graduated to hurting humans, so Rico wanted to turn him in. But reporting the incident to the police wouldn't do any good without some kind of physical description or a name.

As Molly soothed the poor, frightened critter, Rico raked a hand through his hair. They couldn't very well turn that dog loose. The psycho guy would probably just find him again and tie him to another car.

"I'll talk to someone in the restaurant," Rico said, "and ask them to call the pound."

"Oh, no you won't." She looked at him as though he'd suggested something ludicrous and clutched the dog close to her breast. "This little guy is not going anywhere." Then she turned her attention to the scraggly mutt. "Don't you worry, sweetie. I won't let anyone hurt you."

Now, how in the hell was she planning to protect…?

Uh-oh. The flicker of a lightbulb went on in his mind. "I hope you're not planning on keeping that dog. We're staying in a hotel, remember?"

"I'm *not* leaving him on the street and he's *not* going to the pound."

Rico placed his hands on his hips, making a stand. "Well, he's not coming with us."

She lifted her chin, defiance blazing in those pretty green eyes. "Then I'll have to take a cab back to the hotel."

For a woman who walked with her head in the clouds most of the time, she sure had a lot of spunk. And even though she was flat-out defying him—something he damn sure wasn't used to—he couldn't help but admire her at the same time.

Oblivious to the stain on her blouse, she lifted the little dog to eye level. "I've got shampoo, conditioner and a blow-dryer back at the hotel. And in no time at all you'll be spic and span, Petey."

"You've named him already?"

She nodded. "Yes, after the little dog who woke Lori and me during the fire in our apartment."

The stray she'd been forced to give up.

She was thinking with her heart, not her head. "What are you trying to do? Replace a dog you lost?"

There went that proud little chin again, lifting in determination as her gaze drilled deep inside of him. "Aren't you the guy who traced an old Corvette? And just who or what were you trying to replace?"

Her words—and their accuracy—knocked the wind out of his sails, driving away any reasonable argument he could supply.

Or any words at all, for that matter.

"Why don't you tell Maria we'd like our food boxed to go," she suggested. "We can't take Petey into Rosa-rita's."

He wanted to argue about taking the dog anywhere but figured it was easier to give in. Molly was proving to be one stubborn woman, especially when she set her sights on something, like finding her sister or taking in strays.

As it was, he turned and headed for the front door of the restaurant, grumbling as he went.

"And will you please order something that Petey can eat?" she called to his back. "Maybe a side of chicken or beef?"

Rico swore under his breath. It's not as though Rico expected her to let the dog starve. But what was wrong with feeding it table scraps? She was making a special request for the mutt as if it had a champion pedigree.

By the time Rico returned to the car with two bags containing their food, Petey Junior had gotten Molly's white blouse grungy. Her cheek, too. But she was oblivious to everything but the damn dog.

All the way back to the hotel she fed it scraps of spicy shredded beef, something that was bound to upset a stray, hungry dog's stomach. And that was bound to have some big repercussions, especially for the carpet in her hotel room.

But oh, no. Mollyanna wouldn't care about that.

Her loyalty to the stray was tough to comprehend.

She glanced across the console and caught Rico looking at her.

"You won't be sorry," she said.

"I'm already sorry. That little dog smells like he's been Dumpster diving. And he'll probably get a case of the runs from eating that spicy meat you're feeding him."

"Yes, but wait until you see how cute he is after his bath."

"After handling that mutt, you're going to need a bath, too."

For some dumb reason, his mind drifted to the tub in his hotel room, to Molly standing naked under the showerhead, the water streaming down her back. To Rico beside her, applying shampoo to her hair...

Oh, hell. What was he thinking? All he needed to do was let his hormones have free rein, especially with a woman like Molly. She'd be the kind of lover who wanted more of him than he could offer. A whole lot more.

And he wasn't the kind of guy who would trot two steps behind a woman, dutifully nodding and saying, "Yes, dear."

So why couldn't he just focus on that and tell his libido to take a flying leap?

Rico parked near the rear entrance of the hotel and watched as the crazy woman fumbled with the buttons on her blouse. "What in the hell are you doing?"

"I have to sneak him inside." She continued her work,

flashing the white lace of her bra and the swell of her breasts, taunting him, making him rethink his decision about not having sex with her.

Heck, you never knew. She didn't appear to be particularly modest right now. Maybe she *would* be agreeable to a no-strings-attached love affair. A one-shot sexual encounter that would knock their socks off, as well as quell that damned attraction once and for all.

She slipped the dog inside her blouse, then buttoned it up to the top. "Now, be quiet, Petey. I'll let you down as soon as we get into my room."

Rico merely shook his head as he followed her through a side door of the hotel and into an open elevator.

When she reached her room, she fumbled for the key, opened the door and stepped inside. Then she turned and looked at Rico with a smug glimmer in her eyes.

His gaze dropped to her chest, where a terrier-size lump moved, causing the grungy smudge on her blouse to sway and wiggle.

"You know," he said, nodding to the stain, "that'll probably never come out."

"I don't care. Will you please save my tostada for me? I'm going to get Petey cleaned up before I eat."

"Whatever," Rico muttered as he let himself in his own room.

An hour later a light knock sounded at the door that linked their two rooms.

He opened it and nearly dropped his jaw. But not just

because Molly had changed into a white curve-hugging dress, smelled shower-fresh and shot him a heart-stopping smile.

She held a small, tricolored terrier mutt, its coat clean and combed, its eyes bright, its little pink tongue panting.

"Isn't he darling?" she asked. "I knew a bath would make a big difference."

Rico hated to admit it, but the dog had been transformed from a mangy mutt to beloved pet.

"What do you think?" she asked.

He slowly shook his head. "I think that if you ever get tired of planning weddings, you'd make a heck of a dog groomer. I can't believe that's the same animal."

"It's amazing what a little shampoo and conditioner will do," she said.

And a little faith, hope and love, Rico thought.

Molly placed Petey on the floor, assuming he'd go back to sniffing around his new surroundings. But the dog zipped past a barefoot Rico and rushed into the adjoining room, obviously intent on exploring further.

"Hey," she called to Petey. "Come back here. You weren't invited in there."

Rico stepped aside, and she followed Petey, just in time to see the dog grab one of Rico's loafers and make a mad dash under the bed.

"Uh-oh." Petey was going to be in big trouble. She

expected those were expensive shoes—probably Italian leather.

She knelt beside Rico's bed, near the edge of the mattress, and hiked up the spread. She spotted Petey near the headboard and *way* out of arm's reach.

"You're going to have to help me," she said, glancing over her shoulder and looking at Rico.

But he wasn't focused on her face, on her voice. He was looking at her rear end, and she'd just plopped down without thinking about the dress she was wearing. As she sneaked a peek at her behind, she saw that her hem had risen dangerously high, revealing way too much skin.

"Oops." She tugged the fabric back in place. "Sorry."

"No problem."

Maybe not, but there was an intensity in his expression, a hunger in his eye.

"I…uh…need some help," she said.

"What kind of help?"

She blew out a frustrated sigh. "Just look at him. He's right there, between the headboard and the nightstand. And I can't reach him."

Rico joined her on the floor and peered under the bed. "Damn. He's really chomping on my shoe."

They had to come up with some kind of a game plan to get the dog out.

As Molly started to back away from the bed, Rico did, too. But their shoulders bumped and their arms brushed, sending a flood of warmth fluttering through her veins and shining a new light on her dreams.

Their eyes met and something swirled around them, something strong and binding. Something wild and reckless.

She didn't dare move, didn't dare breathe.

His gaze, clouded with desire, challenged her to do something, to make the first move.

"I don't know what we've been skating around," she admitted. "But it's getting too hard to ignore."

"That's for sure." He sat back, resting his butt against his heels.

She did the same. "So what are we going to do about it?"

"There's only one thing I can think of."

Anticipation swept through her chest, setting her senses on alert and her heart on edge, until he pulled her into his arms. And right there, kneeling on the floor beside the bed, he kissed her.

As she surrendered to temptation, to the desire, to the powerful sexual pull that had been building since the first day they laid eyes on each other, Molly knew her life would never be the same again.

Their tongues mated, and Rico caressed her back, sliding one hand over her hip and down the side of her leg to the place where the hem of her dress touched her thigh. His fingers slipped under the fabric, branding her skin and stoking a fire deep inside.

She ached for more of his touch, for more of him.

They could easily get carried away, taking their passion to the floor or up on the bed.

Is that what she wanted?

Her body certainly did.

He tore his mouth from hers but held her close as he whispered, "Molly, you're driving me wild. And it makes it hard to be reasonable."

Then he kissed her again, hotter this time, deeper, and sending her mind spinning out of control.

She wanted him, wanted this so badly she ached deep inside. But not just in her feminine core, in the very heart of her.

A sudden realization swept over her, telling her it was more than passion drawing her to Rico, more than lust.

It was love.

In spite of all her hopes and carefully made plans, she'd fallen heart over dreams for Rico Garcia, a man *so* not her type. A man who didn't have many of the qualities she'd expected her prince to have yet seemed to possess all the ones she needed.

Her first impulse was to intensify the kiss, to begin removing clothing. But if she was going to lay her heart and dreams on the line, Rico needed to know why.

She pulled her mouth from his, her breaths coming out in soft but ragged little pants. "I didn't mean for this to happen."

"Neither did I."

Oh, God. Was he talking about the kiss? Or had he fallen in love with her, too?

It sure seemed like it.

Someone had to admit it, had to say it. And it was obvious—at least, to her—that she was the stronger of the two, more in touch with her feelings.

So she placed a gentle hand on his face, felt the light bristle on his cheek, the strong angle of his jaw. "I love you."

Molly's words slammed into Rico like a speeding Mack truck. His heart skipped into panic mode, trying to break free. To escape.

She loved him?

That wasn't supposed to happen. They'd just shared a kiss or two. Just a little innocent sexual foreplay.

It had been Rico's libido at work, not his brain—and definitely not his heart.

Hell, he'd merely been awestruck by the way the fabric of her dress stretched across her hips, by the nicely rounded bottom she'd aimed in his direction, by the sight of her upper thigh, the glimpse of her panties.

And when he'd gotten down on the floor next to her, it had been the glimmer in her eye, the way her tongue had licked her top lip, the fragrance of peach blossoms, the peppermint scent of her toothpaste.

A rush of testosterone had taken over from there, tossing him right into the middle of the sticky wicket he was facing now.

Before he could think or respond, his cell phone rang, saving him from sure and sudden emotional death.

"I…uh…better get that."

She nodded, yet he could see the disappointment in her face as she realized he'd chosen to answer the phone rather than address her "I love you."

But hell, that's why he didn't date women like her, why he never had to discuss things like love and commitment.

He stood and made his way to the desk, where his phone rested. He glanced at the display, noting a local number he didn't recognize. Then he flipped open the lid and spoke into the receiver. "Hello?"

"Mr. Garcia?" a young woman's voice asked.

"Yes?"

"This is Lori Miller. I heard that you were looking for me and that you know where I can find my sister."

A burst of light flashed before him, the welcome glow at the end of a long black tunnel he'd found himself in, and he released a pent-up sigh.

The case was coming to an end and he could break free of the hold Molly had on him.

"That's right," he told Lori. "Hang on, I'll get her." He handed his cell to Molly. "It's for you."

He probably should have given her a heads-up, but for some reason he felt compelled to sit back and watch the surprise unfold on her face, in her voice.

"Hello?" She appeared to make a quick flick of her mental rolodex, trying to recognize the voice. "Yes?"

Time seemed to stop, then joy exploded on her face. "Oh, my God. Lori! I can't believe it. Where are you? When can I see you?"

Rico waited, wishing he could hear both sides of the conversation.

"All right. Let me get a pen." She spun to the right, then the left, as if her mind couldn't keep up with her heart.

"It's on the desk," Rico told her, unable to hold back a silly grin.

"We'll be right there," she told her sister. "Please don't move."

She shoved the notepad at Rico, then went in search of her shoes. It was almost comical to watch, and if she hadn't been so damn cute, he might have grabbed her by the shoulders and told her to slow down, to get it together.

But the fact was, he was afraid to touch her. Afraid to deal with the "I love you" she'd tossed at him. And afraid to get too close to her again, to touch her. To kiss her. To fall under a subtle, rose-colored enchantment, a spell that was sure to weaken him.

Molly laughed at something, and Rico wondered if she'd forgotten about the words she'd said or if she realized she'd been caught up in a heady fog of lust and hadn't meant them. He hoped so.

Either way, he was almost home free. All he had to do was deliver Molly to her sister, then figure out a way to get his bachelor ass back to Manhattan.

But not without his shoe.

Where the hell was that dog?

After moving the nightstand to the side—and pre-pared to tilt the bed on end if he had to—he reached under the frame and latched on to his loafer with a fin-ger. Following a brief but ineffective tug-of-war with Petey, Rico came out the winner.

He studied the little teeth marks and doggy drool on his Cole Haan.

Petey was going to be a *real* handful. Thank good-ness the rascally little pup wouldn't be Rico's concern.

Not much longer, anyway.

When Molly disconnected the line, she flashed a happy smile. "Lori is waiting for me at the Sleepytime Lodge, a motel on Seventh and Ash not far from the apartment where we used to live."

"Then let's go."

She headed for the door.

"Hey," Rico said. "What about the dog?"

"What about him?"

"Are you planning to leave him here? Alone?"

"I'm afraid to take him with me. I doubt the Sleepy-time Lodge is any more pet-friendly than this place. Be-sides, we're meeting at the diner connected to the motel, and it would be difficult to sneak him in there."

Surely, she could see that the dog would be better in a kennel and not with them. "What if he pees on the carpet?"

"I'll report it to housekeeping and pay for them to bring in a steam cleaner."

"And what if he…?" Rico blew out a sigh. Other damages wouldn't bother her either. She probably planned to pay for them, too. "Oh, never mind. Let's go find your sister."

Molly grabbed her purse, and Rico snatched the car keys from the nightstand, knowing this meeting was his saving grace.

His way out.

He'd lived up to his commitment. He'd helped Molly find her sister. Now he could ride off into the sunset.

Alone.

## Chapter Thirteen

Molly hurried into the small restaurant that sat just off the hotel lobby of the Sleepytime Lodge while Rico parked the car.

She quickly scanned the dining room for a young blonde in her late teens. She'd been waiting twelve years for this, and her dream had finally come true.

A tall young woman with chin-length black hair approached, her blue eyes glimmering. "Molly?"

"Yes?"

"It's me. Lori."

Molly narrowed her gaze, checking out the dark locks, trying to recognize a glimpse of the child her sister had once been, trying to make sure this wasn't some kind of hoax. Was this really her?

"I colored my hair," the young woman said. "And I cut it, too. It was my friend Becky's idea. After I ran away, she thought it would help hide my appearance. And…well, I sort of like it."

Recognition dawned, and Molly drew her sister into a hug. "Oh, Lori. I can't believe it's really you. You have no idea how badly I've wanted to find you."

"Yes, I do. I've really missed you, too."

"Sorry for interrupting," Rico said as he walked into the diner, reached out a hand to Lori and introduced himself. Then he handed Molly the keys. "When you're ready to head back to the hotel, take the car. I'll walk."

"Are you sure?" Molly asked.

"Yep. Three of us won't fit inside anyway. And I could use a little fresh air."

For a moment she wanted to take him aside, to ask him about the conversation they'd started at the hotel, especially since he'd talked nonstop about Lori on the drive over there.

"Have fun," Rico said.

She appreciated his thoughtfulness and flashed him a smile as she placed the keys in her purse. "Thanks, we'll see you later."

As Rico walked out of the diner, Molly motioned for the hostess, indicating she wanted to be served. "I'll get us a table."

Moments later she and Lori were seated at a small booth and waiting for the waitress to bring them two sodas. They'd been close in the past, but an awkwardness settled over them.

"Were the Millers good to you?" Molly asked.

"Yeah, but when I moved in with them, it was really hard. I was so scared."

"It nearly killed me to watch them take you away and not be able to do anything about it."

"I know that now. At first, I couldn't understand why you didn't come and get me. You had always taken such good care of me. But after a while, I figured it out. My mom and dad—well, the Millers—didn't realize how close we were, how cruel it had been to separate us." Lori placed her hands on the table and leaned forward. "But what about you? Did you get adopted?"

"No, not officially." Molly told her about the Townsends, about how she'd like Lori to meet them someday.

A lot went unspoken, yet shared emotions—like grief, relief and love—hovered over them, reminding them of the closeness they'd shared.

"I know you've had issues with your stepmother," Molly said. "But was your adoptive mom good to you? I'd hoped and prayed she would be."

Lori nodded. "Yeah, she was. I think it was her idea to adopt me, so she tried hard to be a good mother and to make me happy. You know, by baking cookies and taking me to the park. She loved me, and I loved her, too."

Molly was so glad to hear it.

"It was pretty tough when she died, but at least my dad and I had each other." Lori clicked her tongue. "Until he married the wicked witch of the Twin Cities. Her name is Sierra and she's just a couple of years older than I am. She moved right into my mother's house, throwing away things that held a sentimental value for Dad and me, buying new furniture and changing everything. My dad didn't do a darn thing about it."

"Is that why you ran away?"

"Yeah. And because if I ever argued with her, she'd flutter her lashes at my dad, and he'd always take her side. A couple of times she smacked me, but I knew better than to try and defend myself. She always had a way of making me be the bad guy. So I eventually got fed up with it and took off."

"Your father is worried sick," Molly said.

She paled. "Really?"

Well, at least according to Cowboy he was, so Molly nodded.

"Does he know where I am?" Lori asked.

"No, not yet. You don't have to go home, but I think you ought to call and tell him that you're safe."

"You're probably right."

Molly reached across the table, taking her sister's hand. "You can live with me if you want to. I'd love to have you."

Lori brightened. "That would be way cool. Especially since I haven't found a job yet and only have enough money for a couple more nights at this place."

Molly wasn't sure what Rico would say to that, since they hadn't had a chance to discuss their feelings, let alone the future. But she would talk to him later.

Right now she was curious about Lori, about her sister's past. "Becky told me you lived in her cabin. What made you decide to come looking for me?"

"While I was out in the boonies, I kept having this dream about a fire, about being trapped and scared. At first I thought it was because I was alone, with no one to talk to, no way of knowing if I was safe and afraid that if I died no one would ever know. But then I decided it was the apartment fire that triggered my dreams. And that I'd better come to grips with my past so I could deal with the present."

After they were through with rehashing the past, Molly looked forward to talking to Lori about the future, about dreams and going to college.

But there was time for that kind of pep talk later, after they'd caught up on twelve years.

And after Molly and Rico got a chance to discuss their own future.

It didn't take Rico too long to get back to the Starlight Palms. On the way he'd called Margie, catching her just before she left the office to go home. He asked her to get him a flight out of Los Angeles tonight—on a red-eye if necessary. He was eager to pack his bags and return to Manhattan, ready to get his life back on track. But he wouldn't leave Molly in a pinch.

He planned to take a cab to the airport, leaving the rental car with her. And he'd tell her she and her sister could keep the hotel rooms for the next couple of days. He'd even spring for the charges.

Maybe, while in the midst of her reunion with Lori, Molly would forget about the kisses she and Rico had shared, forget about the love she'd confessed.

He sure hoped so.

Whatever it was that he'd been feeling for her scared the hell out of him. It wasn't love, though. It couldn't be that.

As he let himself into his room, Petey came running to greet him.

"Hey, mutt." Rico scooped up the rascally pup and rubbed his ears. "Have you been staying out of trouble?"

Petey nuzzled Rico's cheek with his wet nose, then slapped a lick across his chin. He was a cute little guy.

Aw, hell, Rico thought as he put the dog back on the floor. Even Petey was starting to grow on him.

It didn't take long to pack his bags. And moments later Margie called with his itinerary. It was going to be a heck of a flight, with a layover in Chicago. And he wouldn't get to JFK until nine in the morning.

He glanced at his watch, realizing he still had plenty

of time. But he may as well hang out at the airport rather than here.

Okay, so he was running scared.

He always tried to be honest with the women he dated, polite. But things had gotten a little out of hand with Molly, who wasn't just any woman. She was his mom's friend. And what was worse, Rico actually had begun to like her.

A lot.

And he didn't want to hurt her.

After checking with the hotel desk clerk, he paid for their stay to date, then guaranteed any charges Molly might have in the next couple of days.

"Can you call me a cab?" he asked the bellman. "I'll go get my bag."

"Certainly, sir. It may take a few minutes. I called for another guest, and it took nearly a half hour to get here."

"No problem."

As Rico headed back to his room. He wasn't going to just skip out entirely. He planned to leave Molly a note telling her he had to leave unexpectedly and asking her to call him.

When he let himself in, Petey met him at the door, barked a greeting, then began to sniff around the floor.

Uh-oh.

"Hold on, buddy. I'll see if I can find a better place for a doggy constitutional." Rico picked up the little mutt, wrapped him in a bath towel, then snuck him out the side door to a patch of dirt and grass behind the hotel.

He set Petey down so he could pee or whatever.

For a moment he worried Molly's pet might run off—a major catastrophe for sure—but the dog didn't stray very far.

It looked as though Petey knew a good thing when he had it. When he'd finished his doggy business, he ran to Rico, wagging his tail.

"Come on, sport." Rico scooped him up, wrapped him back in the towel, then carried him back inside.

As Petey scampered around the room, Rico wrote a note to Molly and left it on the pillow of her bed. Then he grabbed his carry-on bag and opened the door. But before he could step into hall, he spotted Molly and Lori coming his way.

Molly waved, her eyes bright, causing his heart to rumble in his chest.

"Hey," Rico said as he held the door open for them. "I've got to head back to New York this evening, so I'll leave the rental car with you. I've already taken care of the room for another couple of days, just in case you'd like to stay here."

"Oh, my gosh," Lori said, spotting Petey in the open doorway. "What a cute little dog."

Rico clutched the handle his carry-on bag until his knuckles ached. "I'm afraid business calls," he told Molly. "I have a cab waiting out front."

The glimmer in Molly's eye faded a tad.

"It was nice meeting you," Rico told Lori.

"Same here," the young woman said as she continued to play with Petey.

"I'll walk out with you," Molly said.

What could he say?

They continued along the hall in silence for a while, but he wasn't sure what to do about it. Words might only confuse the issue.

Molly already had his head spinning, his pulse throbbing. And all he could think of was making a quick getaway.

"Everything worked out so well," she said. "And I have you to thank. I doubt Lori or I would have found each other without you."

"No problem. To be honest, it was worth every bit of my time just to see the joy on your face when you talked to her for the first time." Oh, for cripes sake. It was true, but could it have come out any mushier than that?

Molly was doing a real number on him, making him soft already. And the sooner he got on his way, the better.

"I wish you didn't have to go tonight," she said.

"Hey, you know how it is." He flashed her a phony smile, one that went with the BS he was dishing out, the guilt he was feeling about his mad dash to freedom.

"We didn't get a chance to discuss it," she told him. "But I meant what I said, Rico. I love you."

Damn.

She might think he was the one she'd been waiting for, but he always avoided women like Molly.

He needed to pull back, put some distance between them, grow more focused on his work, on the need to get back to New York. Then maybe his association with Molly would finally be severed.

"I'm not the kind of man who deserves a woman like you."

"Don't sell yourself short," she said, with her trademark Pollyanna smile. "There's more to you than meets the eye."

She'd better not look too close. Even Rico didn't like what he saw sometimes, especially now, when it was tearing him up to spit out the words that needed to be said. "I don't feel the same way about you, Molly."

The emotion in her eyes nearly knocked him to his knees, but he couldn't quit now, couldn't weaken. He had to make this quick and easy, like jumping into a cold stream or tearing off a bandage.

"You don't love me?" she asked. "Not even a little?"

Yes. No. Maybe.

Hell, he didn't know. But even if he did, this wouldn't work. Not for him.

"No, I don't love you." He wouldn't allow himself to.

Expecting her to fall apart, to weep and cling to him, he watched as a single tear trailed down her cheek.

She lifted her chin, swiped it away, then turned on her heel and walked away.

He had the urge to go after her, to tell her they ought

to talk about it later, after they had some time to think through things.

But he didn't.

She'll be okay, he told himself. She had her sister to keep her happy, a dog to cuddle and a dream mate to wait for—someone more her type than Rico.

He ought to thank his lucky stars that he'd gotten away scot-free.

But for some damn reason, he didn't feel like celebrating.

Three days after leaving Molly in Los Angeles, Rico paced the floor of his Manhattan office, struggling to stay seated at his desk and write a report that was due tomorrow.

In fact, his trip to California had really set him back, and he'd returned to find himself up to his butt in deadlines and facing several problems that no one else in the office knew how to deal with.

Normally he did his best work under pressure, but he seemed to have lost his focus—something that never happened to him.

But then again, he'd never obsessed about a woman before either. Never let thoughts of a pretty blonde with a radiant smile interrupt him at work.

The only thing on his mind was Molly and the hold she still had on him, a hold that time and separation hadn't lessened.

He'd expected her to call, to plead with him. To beg him to reconsider the love she'd offered, to prod him to think about his feelings for her.

And he'd expected to feel a sharp stab of guilt when she did, since the way he'd left had gone against his grain and hadn't been fair to her.

But she *hadn't* called. And now he was beginning to think she might not.

There was a strength in her he hadn't recognized, a stubborn determination he'd neglected to see.

The day before yesterday he'd received his closing statement from the Starlight Palms by fax. Apparently on the afternoon he'd left, Molly had checked out of the room he'd stayed in. And the next morning she'd checked out of hers.

But there'd been no direct contact, no messages. Nothing.

He ought to be happy about that, but for some reason he wasn't. He felt as though he owed her something. An explanation maybe. A better ending for a relationship that really hadn't even gotten off the ground.

She was probably busy with her sister, which was a good thing. Having her mind occupied with Lori would help her get over him. But something niggled at him. And he'd be damned if he knew what it was.

The fact he'd hurt her feelings, probably. Even if she hadn't called.

Hell, he didn't hurt women, didn't make them cry.

That's why he'd always kept his relationships casual. Light and insignificant.

And that's what he'd meant to do with Molly.

It was weird, though. Even though they hadn't slept together, a relationship had still developed. And it had deepened to something significant.

Go figure.

Out of habit, he pulled open his bottom desk drawer and spotted an open bag of bite-size Snickers. He reached for one, then let the candy drop back into the plastic sack. Hell, even his favorite sweets weren't doing the trick.

A light rap sounded at the door.

"Come on in."

Margie stepped inside. "I'm running down to the Italian deli on the corner. Do you want me to pick up one of those meatball sandwiches for you?"

"No, thanks. I'm okay." He'd had a muffin for breakfast. He glanced at the right side of his desk, where a pretty good-size chunk remained. All right, so he'd had half of a muffin. "My appetite hasn't been that great the past couple of days."

"That's not like you. You're always hungry."

Maybe he was coming down with some bug he'd picked up on the airplane. He actually hoped so, which was a stupid thing to wish for. But the alternative didn't sit well with him.

"This doesn't have anything to do with the blonde you took to Los Angeles, does it?"

"How'd you know she was blonde?" he asked.

"Cowboy calls in when he's on assignment, too."

He clucked his tongue. "She was a client." ·

"Oh, yeah? Then why haven't you given me a billing report?"

"This case was gratis. She was a friend of my mom's."

Margie cracked a grin and her eyes glimmered. "Your mom is the one who told me you'd prefer to have adjoining rooms."

"My mom?" Rico frowned. "She's in Europe."

"I know. But she called from Munich to let you know they'd arrived safely. And when I told her you'd gone to meet Cowboy on a case, she asked if you'd taken a Molly Townsend with you. And I said…"

"Okay, okay. So my mom was playing matchmaker from abroad, telling you my pretty blond companion was a perfect match."

Margie chuckled. "She mentioned the perfect match. But Cowboy told me Molly was blond. So I figured you'd appreciate the adjoining rooms."

"I didn't."

She arched a brow. "Come now. Don't tell me that Rico Garcia struck out."

Actually he'd purposely hit a ground ball to first, sacrificing for the sake of the home team.

"Your silence is answer enough for me. You're in love and brokenhearted."

"The hell I am." Just the thought that he might be lovesick sent a wave of panic through his gut. But he couldn't help wondering if Molly had somehow left an imprint on his heart.

He glanced out the window, scanning the neighboring buildings. A flock of birds. A nondescript cloud formation. Anything to keep from turning back and facing Margie's assessing gaze.

"Well," Margie said, "if you don't mind, I'll head to the deli. Can you answer the phones while I'm out?"

"Sure."

When Margie left, Rico raked a hand through his hair, hoping it would dislodge the memory of Molly's smile, the lilt of her laugh, the challenge of her optimism, the heat of her kiss.

If anyone could make Rico take a chance on love, it would be the pretty blond bridal consultant who'd turned his life inside out the moment he'd met her.

But that didn't mean he'd be fool enough to continue seeing her, to risk his heart and fall in love, to make a commitment to her and accept the happy-ever-after philosophy she promoted.

Or did it?

## Chapter Fourteen

Molly's heart had been crushed when Rico told her he didn't love her. And his quick departure had left her hurting.

But she'd forced herself to go back to her hotel room, back to Lori, and try to make the best of things.

She'd been thrilled to have her sister back, but a black hole remained in her heart, in her life.

Rico was missing.

After checking out of the hotel, she and Lori stopped at a discount store and headed for the pet section, where they bought a little red collar and leash, doggy toys, food and a special carrier they could use to take Petey on the airplane.

Then they all flew to New York, with Petey traveling as a carry-on.

On their first night home Lori had called Sam Miller to let him know she was safe and would be staying with Molly for a while. The man had been elated to hear her voice, and Lori had suspected that he'd actually gotten a little teary-eyed.

According to Lori, the man hadn't realized how unhappy she'd been and was eager to mend their fences. He'd also asked if it was all right for him to come out to visit in the next month—alone. He wanted to get their father-daughter relationship back on track, saying they'd deal with the stepmother issue later.

Afterward Molly had called the Townsends and shared the news of the sisters' reunion. Her parents had been overjoyed, since they knew how dearly Molly loved Lori and how badly she'd missed her. Now both Lori and Molly would be flying to Florida over the Fourth of July weekend.

In the meantime, while fixing up the spare bedroom for Lori, the sisters made up for lost time, getting to know each other again.

All in all, the past two days had gone by exceptionally well. But the nights were another story.

Molly had found it hard to sleep, hard to think of anything but Rico, the love she'd offered him and his rejection.

She'd tried to tell herself that he felt something for

her, too, that he was running scared. But it didn't seem to help.

He'd been stone-cold clear and had broken her heart. And she doubted it would mend anytime soon—if at all.

Each time the cynical P.I. came to mind—which was far more often than Molly liked—she would try to conjure an image of her ideal man: a Brad Pitt look-alike with Don Townsend's heart of gold.

But it hadn't worked.

It was Rico she loved, Rico she wanted.

And in her disappointment she'd learned a hard lesson, a truth Rico had warned her about.

Falling in love didn't guarantee a happy ever after.

Today had been Molly's first day back at work, but she'd only gone through the motions. Her job no longer excited her. And the happy brides only reminded her of how lonely she'd become—even with a sister and a pet waiting at home.

She glanced at her watch. It was after five. Betty and the other salesclerks had gone home for the day, leaving Molly to lock up the bridal boutique.

As she prepared to check her schedule for tomorrow, she glanced behind her at the rack behind the counter of dresses that had already been purchased.

Susan Sullivan's gown, the princess-style Vera Wang, hung in front. It had already been altered and was waiting to be pressed and packed with tissue so the bride could take it home.

It was beautiful, not to mention a six, the same size Molly wore.

She took it down, then carried it to the mirror and held it in front of her. As she studied her reflection, she imagined herself as a bride.

It was a silly game she'd played in the past when no one was around. And it had always bolstered her dream and reinforced her belief that things always worked out for the best.

Would the game improve her mood this evening?

It certainly couldn't hurt.

Molly took the expensive gown to a dressing room, then slowly undressed, placing her folded clothing on the chair.

As she stepped into Susan's gown, she hoped to shed her Rico-induced sadness and regain her dreams, her hope that someday there'd be another man, another love.

She tried to button the back of her dress the best she could, then lifted her skirts and swept into the front of the shop, where she stopped in front of a full-length mirror.

The shoulders of the gown bunched in back because she hadn't been able to reach all the tiny buttons or the small hidden zipper. So she sucked in her breath and, while twisting and tugging, managed to get herself put together.

There. That was better.

The elegant dress had cost Susan's father nearly ten thousand dollars.

And even though Molly looked like a princess in the stunning gown, she felt like a pauper on the inside, in spite of conjuring the required here-comes-the-bride smile.

But she just couldn't seem to fake happiness. Not today.

Still, the dress was beautiful.

She glanced at the clock on the wall. Twenty-seven minutes after five. Time to stop her childish game of pretend and go home before she got the dress dirty—or, God forbid, perspired while wearing it.

She reached in back and struggled to undo the buttons, but when she reached the zipper, it wouldn't budge.

Oh, dang. It was stuck.

If she pulled, she could rip something.

Panic swirled in her chest. She had to get the dress off, had to get it back on the hanger.

She closed her eyes, taking a slow, steady breath. Relax. Don't sweat....

*Oh, dear God. This is awful.*

*Think, Molly. Think.*

Nothing.

A knock sounded at the glass door of the shop, sending her senses reeling and making her afraid to turn to the side, to take a peek and see who it might be.

Was it Betty?

Had she forgotten something?

Oh, man. Her boss would absolutely flip if she saw an employee wearing a customer's gown. Of course, she'd also help Molly get the darn zipper undone.

But what if it was Susan Sullivan at the door?

That would be so much worse than seeing Betty.

The knock on the door grew louder, more insistent.

"Open up," the muffled sound of a familiar baritone hollered.

*Rico.*

Molly spun around and saw him standing beyond the glass.

He was a sight for sore eyes, and just his presence alone seemed to turn her knees to Silly Putty. But he looked mesmerized, and it appeared as though a whisper might blow him over.

A part of her hoped he was bowled over by the sight of her.

Of course, he was probably just dumbstruck by her crazy plight.

She didn't know if she should laugh or cry. Either way, she'd better drag him in and have him help her.

As she unlocked the door, he stepped inside and waited while she secured the entrance to the shop again. No way did she want anyone coming in and seeing what she'd done.

When she turned around, Rico darn near gaped at her, which she supposed was understandable.

"What are you doing?" he asked.

She'd been pretending, but she certainly wouldn't admit that. A lie came to mind, causing her cheeks to heat, but that wasn't going to stop her from protecting her embarrassing secret activity. "Susan Sullivan is about my size, and I wanted to make sure this dress would fit. It just came back from alterations."

He nodded, accepting her answer. Yet his eyes continued to study her, the gown. "Your sister told me I could find you here."

Rico had been looking for her?

Well, of course. Why else would he come to the bridal shop?

Molly didn't dare breathe, let alone speak.

As his gaze slowly swept the length of her again— up, down and back—he wore the whisper of a smile. "You look beautiful."

"Thank you." Her cheeks continued to burn.

"I need to tell you something," he said.

She couldn't imagine what, but his presence was heating the room. And if her nervousness continued, she'd start sweating like a guilty criminal and land herself in a real jam.

"Can it wait?" she asked.

His smile disappeared. "No, it's been too long coming."

An apology? she wondered. For being so abrupt the day she'd told him that she loved him? The day he'd thrown her heart back in her face?

He took her hand, brushed his thumb across her skin,

sending a shiver of heat through her veins and causing her heart to spin, her hope to soar.

"I love you, Mollyanna." His gaze reached deep inside of her.

"Are you sure?"

He placed a hand on her jaw, and his thumb caressed her cheek. "I fought it every step of the way, but I was no match for you. From the moment I spotted your loyalty to Lori and your determination to find her again, I began to buckle. And when I saw how your love and faith transformed Petey from an unwanted stray to a cherished pet, I knew I wanted you in my corner." Then he dropped to one knee. "You'll never find a man more in need of your love than me. Will you marry me?"

His words, his sweet proposal, knocked the breath right out of her.

"Aren't you going to say something?" he asked, looking up at her with desperation in his eyes.

She blinked back tears of joy and swallowed hard. "From the day you stepped out of that vintage Corvette, I was afraid to believe I'd been waiting for you all my life. But it's true."

"I'm far from perfect," he admitted. "And I'm not sure I deserve a woman like you."

"I've had my heart set on perfect for as long as I can remember, but it's not perfection I need. It's you, Rico." Then she pulled him to his feet and wrapped her arms around his neck. "Yes, I'll marry you."

As Rico lowered his head to place his mouth on hers, Molly gasped, then pushed against his chest. "Oh, no. Wait!"

He couldn't imagine what had put a damper on the kiss he'd been longing for. "What's the matter?"

"You've got to get me out of this dress."

Making love in the back room of a bridal shop would be a first, and his lips quirked in a crooked smile.

"It's not funny." Molly grabbed his hand and drew him to a dressing room. "I'm stuck in this gown and can't get out."

"You've got to be kidding."

"Nope. I was playing dress-up, and it backfired."

Rico couldn't help but laugh. "Honey, living with you is bound to be one surprise after another."

She flashed him an impish grin that damn near turned him inside out. "I think that's what they mean by For Better or Worse." Then she turned and presented her back. "There's a little hidden zipper back there and it's snagged on something."

"I see it." He carefully worked at the contraption until a tiny piece of lace was dislodged. "You're free."

Rico watched as she slowly stepped out of the white, billowy garment, revealing a taunting pair of pink lace panties and matching bra.

She carefully hung the gown, and when she turned, facing him, he drank in every bit of her, every perfect inch. Her beauty overwhelmed him, and so did the fact that she would be his for the rest of his life. He cupped her cheeks and drew her mouth to his.

She slipped her arms around his neck, then kissed him senseless.

As his hands slid along the skin of her back, passion flared and testosterone soared. But so did love and the desire to cherish her forever, to take his time and love her the way she deserved. To make their first time special and not to take her in a heated rush in the back room of a bridal shop.

He broke the kiss and brushed a strand of hair from her face. "How long will it take you to plan our wedding?"

"The kind I've been wanting all my life?" she asked.

"You bet. The whole nine yards, including a gown like the one you were wearing."

"Not that one," she said. "It's beautiful, and I love it, but it's too expensive."

"Order it," he said. "And put a rush on it."

"That would take weeks, and to tell you the truth, I'd rather not wait that long."

"Neither would I." In fact, the sooner he got her out of here the better. He handed her the green gypsy-style skirt she'd been wearing, as well as the matching top. "I want you to have the wedding of your dreams. And don't worry about the cost. I'll spring for it all. What else do you want?"

"Lavender tulips," she said, slipping on the blouse. "That is, if I can find a florist who can get them."

"We'll fly them in from Holland, if we have to."

"Rico Garcia…" She paused long enough to put on her skirt, then straightened, crossed her arms and studied him carefully. "I can't believe my ears. I never thought I'd ever see a romantic streak in you."

"Yeah, well get used to it." He brushed a kiss across her brow, then took her by the hand. "Apparently there's been a hopeless romantic living deep inside of me, and loving you has brought him out into the open."

"You won't be sorry," she told him, those green eyes glimmering with a promise.

"For some crazy reason, I think you're right." He ran his knuckles along her cheek. "Come on, let's get out of here."

"Where are we going?" she asked.

"We're going to buy you the biggest diamond ring we can find. Then we're going to call my mother and tell her that her matchmaking skills were a success."

Molly led him out of the shop and locked the door. "I suppose we'll leave my car in the back."

"For the time being." He took her by the hand, and they walked to where he'd parked his rental car. "So now that we've got that settled, there is a condition to all of this."

Molly stopped dead in her tracks. "What kind of condition?"

"You can call all the shots when it comes to the wedding, but I'm in charge of the honeymoon."

She blew out a little sigh of relief. "No problem. It's customary for the groom to handle that."

"Yeah, but is it customary for the groom to insist upon two?"

"You want two honeymoons?"

"Yeah. The first one is going to be tonight. And the second one will be after the ceremony."

Her smile brightened. "I can't think of anything I'd like better."

"Good." Then he picked her up in his arms and kissed her for all the world to see. "I love you, Mollyanna. And tonight, in the bridal suite at the Westlake Inn, I'm going to show you just how much."

"I love you, too, Rico."

He couldn't believe his good fortune. "I never believed in fairytales or happy-ever-afters. Not until I met you."

Then he placed his bride into his car—or rather his chariot—and whisked her off into the sunset, his heart soaring with the promise of a bright and happy future.

\* \* \* \* \*

*Don't miss Judy Duarte's next*
*Silhouette Special Edition,*
*CALL ME COWBOY.*
*Available March 2006.*

# SPECIAL EDITION™

# A LITTLE BIT ENGAGED

## by Teresa Hill

When Kate Cassidy's "perfect" fiancé admitted he loved someone else, her predictable-as-clockwork life turned upside down. Breaking her engagement, she took a pregnant runaway into her home, took the pastor Ben Taylor out on a date—and soon figured out what she really wanted from life....

Available February 2006
from Silhouette Special Edition

Silhouette®

# ┌─SPECIAL EDITION™─┐

# HUSBANDS AND OTHER STRANGERS

by

# Marie Ferrarella

A boating accident left Gayle Elliott Conway with amnesia and no recollection of the handsome man who came to her rescue…her husband. Convinced there was more to the story, Taylor Conway set out for answers and a way back into the heart of the woman he loved.

**Available February 2006**

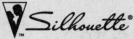

# COMING NEXT MONTH